Fragments of our soul

Kavya Shah

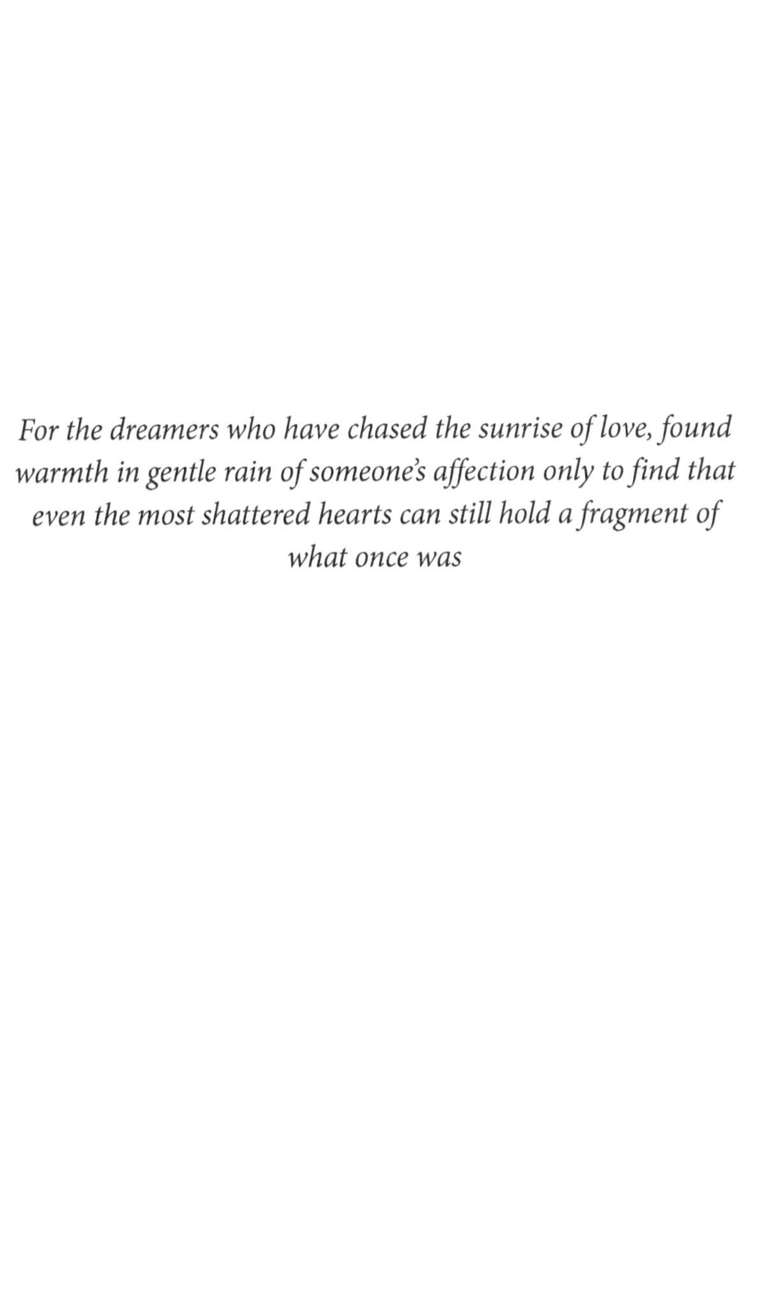

*For the dreamers who have chased the sunrise of love, found
warmth in gentle rain of someone's affection only to find that
even the most shattered hearts can still hold a fragment of
what once was*

The author's envelope

Dear Heart,

As I sit down to share my story with you, I'm filled with a mix of emotions - excitement, vulnerability, and gratitude. You're about to embark on a journey with me, one that's deeply personal, yet universally relatable. It's a journey of love, loss, and self-discovery.

Someone once told me that not everyone reads, that not everyone has the time or the title of "reader." But I believe that's where the magic lies - in the hearts that beat with love, not just in the pages that turn with time. You don't need a label or a schedule to be a part of this journey. All you need is a willingness to feel, to love, and to be loved in return.

That's why I'm not just addressing you as a reader; I'm calling you my dear heart. You're more than just someone who will turn these pages; you're a kindred spirit, a fellow traveler, and a friend. You're the one who will hold my hand through the darkness and the light, who will laugh and cry with me, and who will find solace in the words that follow.

"Fragments of our soul" is more than just a collection of tales of two souls ; it's an invitation to explore the depths of your own heart. It's a reminder that you're not alone in your joys and sorrows, that your emotions are valid, and that your story matters. Within these pages, you'll find fragments of my soul, scattered like autumn leaves, and the whispers of my deepest fears.

This book is a love letter to the human experience, with all its beauty and brutality. It's a celebration of the moments that make us feel alive, and an acknowledgment of the darkness that shapes us. You'll find yourself in these words, in the laughter and the tears, in the moments of triumph and defeat.

As we navigate the seasons of love together, I hope you'll find solace in the words, comfort in the vulnerability, and inspiration in the resilience. You'll discover the enchantment of new love, the intensity of passion, and the comfort of devotion. You'll experience the agony of heartbreak, the struggle to heal, and the triumph of renewal.

You'll realize that love is not just a feeling, but a choice - a choice to be vulnerable, to be open, and to be present. You'll see that love is not just a destination, but a journey - a journey of growth, of self discovery, and of transformation.

So, come with me, dear heart, and let's wander into the wild beauty of love. Let's explore the pathways of our hearts, and discover the hidden corners of our souls. Let's find solace in the words, and comfort in each other's company.

As you read these words, I promise to hold space for you, to listen to your whispers, and to honor your story. I invite you to join a community of hearts that beat with love, compassion, and understanding. Together, let's create a peaceful journey where our stories are cherished, our emotions are validated, and our love is amplified.

And when you turn the final page, I hope you'll realize that the greatest love story is not the one I've written, but the one you've lived - the one that's still unfolding, still beating, and still loving.

With love and vulnerability,
~ Kavya

Contents

Half a decade ago …

Riyan stood at the airport, his eyes fixed on the horizon as if willing the plane to take off. His dark hair, always perfectly messy, framed his chiseled features, softened only by the gentle curve of his lips. The sharp jawline, the piercing gaze, and the quiet confidence that radiated from him like a subtle aura – all of these combined to make Riyan a man who commanded attention without seeking it.

But there was more to Riyan than his chiseled good looks and charming smile. Beneath the polished facade, a whirlpool of emotions churned, hidden from the world like an undertow beneath the surface of a tranquil sea. His eyes, a deep, rich brown, seemed to hold a thousand secrets, each one carefully locked away behind a mask of warmth and concern.

As a child, Riyan had been Kiyana's constant companion, her partner in mischief and adventure. Together, they had explored the hidden corners of their neighborhood, sharing secrets and laughter beneath the shade of ancient trees. But as they grew older, the bond between them remained strong, even as the world around them began to change.

Now, as Riyan prepared to accompany Kiyana to London for her treatment, a mix of emotions swirled within him. His eyes, always so expressive, seemed to cloud for a moment, as if the memories he held within him were threatening to spill over. But then, like a veil drawn over the sun, his expression cleared, leaving only a warm, reassuring smile.

"Hey, Ki," he said, his voice low and smooth, like honey poured over rough stone. "We'll get through this together, okay? You'll be back to your old self in no time."

Kiyana's fragile form leaned into Riyan, her eyes searching for reassurance. Riyan's heart twisted in his chest as he wrapped his arm around her shoulders, holding her close. He knew that some secrets were too fragile to be spoken aloud, some wounds too deep to be healed by words alone. But he also knew that he would do everything in his power to protect Kiyana, to help her regain her memories and rebuild her shattered world.

As they boarded the plane, Riyan's gaze lingered on Kiyana's fragile form, his eyes burning with an intensity that seemed to hold a thousand secrets. And in that moment, it was as if the very fabric of his being seemed to vibrate with a hidden truth, one that only he knew.

Currently...

Kiyana's eyes flew open, her heart racing like crazy. She lay in bed, drenched in sweat, her sheets tangled around her legs like a hold back. The city lights outside her London flat cast a chilling glow on the walls, illuminating the faint scar above her left eyebrow. A dream. It was just a dream. But the memories lingered, haunting her like a ghost from her past. Kiyana's mind was a jumble of fragmented images and emotions, like a puzzle with missing pieces.

In her dream, she was running – her feet pounding the wet pavement, her heart racing with fear. The city lights blurred around her, casting long shadows that seemed to snatch at her clothes. She was desperate to escape, but the darkness closed in, suffocating her.

A soft voice whispered her name. "Kiyana…" It sent shivers down her spine, and for a moment, she felt like she was back in that deserted path, running for her life.

Suddenly, she stumbled, fell, and everything went black. The silence was oppressive, punctuated only by the sound of her own ragged breathing.

Kiyana's gaze drifted around her cozy flat, taking in the familiar photos and dog-eared novels. But despite the comforting surroundings, a sense of unease settled in her stomach, like a cold stone weighing her down.

She threw off the covers and swung her legs over the side of the bed. The scar above her left eyebrow throbbed, a constant reminder of the accident that shattered her memories. Kiyana's eyes narrowed, her mind racing with questions. What had happened that night? Why couldn't she remember?

With trembling fingers, Kiyana reached for her phone and dialed Riyan's number. Her best friend answered on the first ring. "Hey, Ki, what's wrong?" Riyan's voice was laced with concern, but Kiyana detected a hint of wariness beneath the surface. Kiyana took a deep breath, trying to calm her racing heart. "I had a dream," she said, her voice barely above a whisper. "I think it was a memory." Riyan's pause was almost imperceptible. "What did you see?" he asked, his tone cautious. Kiyana closed her eyes, the images still etched in her mind. "I was running," she said. "I was scared. And there was someone calling my name…" The words trailed off, leaving an uncomfortable silence.

As Kiyana waited for Riyan's response, a chill ran down her spine. She felt like she was standing on the edge of a cliff, staring into an empty space of forgotten memories. And she wasn't sure if she was ready to take the leap. Riyan's voice cut through the silence, low and mysterious. "Maybe it's time we talked about your past, Ki." Kiyana's heart skipped a beat. What did Riyan know? And why was he being so cryptic?

The next day…

Kiyana's fingers moved across the canvas, colors blending in a swirling dance. Her art was her refuge, a place where her tangled thoughts could unravel and her emotions could flow freely. The art fair loomed, and she was determined to showcase her best work. Her passion for art and writing had been her constant companions since childhood.

The dream lingered, so vivid and real. Kiyana's mind replayed the fragments: the dark street, the fear, the whisper of her name. Perhaps Riyan was right. Perhaps it was time to face her past. Yet, a deep instinct held her back. She wasn't sure she was ready. She loved her art, and she feared her own thoughts would distract her from her passion.

Just as she was lost in her work, Kiyana's phone buzzed. It was Riyan, her closest friend since childhood. "Hey, Ki! What's up?" Riyan's voice was warm and familiar, with a hint of playfulness.

Kiyana smiled, feeling a sense of comfort. "Just working on a new piece for the art fair. You know how it is. Trying to create something that'll really impress the judges."

Riyan chuckled. "Yeah, I do. And I'm sure you'll amaze them. You're incredibly talented, Ki. Don't ever forget that."

Kiyana's heart warmed with gratitude. Riyan had always been her rock, her confidant. But then, she noticed a slight hesitation in his voice. He was usually so cheerful around her, so she asked, "Riyan, is everything okay?"

Riyan said, "Listen, Ki, I won't lie. There's something about your past you should know. The dream you saw…"

She interrupted, "Riyan, I think we should discuss that after the art fair. I need time to process. I hope you understand."

"Of course, Ki. Right now, nothing is more important than your art fair. We can talk about it later. In fact, Riyan added, his voice reassuring, "don't stress about it too much. It's really not that important. Just a few things that might help you understand your dream. We can go over it after the fair, when you're less busy."

As they chatted, Kiyana's mind drifted. She'd been receiving strange messages lately – cryptic notes and mysterious phone calls. It was as if someone was trying to tell her something, but she couldn't quite understand the message.

Suddenly, she remembered one of the messages: "Your art is more than just colors, Kiyana. It's a doorway to the truth." She felt a flutter in her chest. Who was sending her these messages? And what truth were they talking about?

Riyan's voice brought her back to reality. "Ki, you okay? You spaced out for a second."

Her head shook slightly as she replied to Riyan. "I...I don't know. I'm getting some weird messages these days."

Riyan's voice turned serious. "What did they say?"

Kiyana hesitated, unsure whether to share the message. But something about Riyan's concerned voice put her at ease. "It said...it said my art is a doorway to the truth."

Riyan grew suspicious. "That's creepy. Do you think it's related to the other messages you've been getting?"

Kiyana answered, "I don't know, but I have a feeling it's all connected."

As they talked, Kiyana couldn't shake the feeling that someone was watching her. She glanced around the studio, but there was no one there.

Riyan's voice brought her back to reality. "Ki, let's focus on the art fair for now. We can deal with these weird messages later."

Her nod was lost in the phone connection. She felt a surge of determination. She was going to create something amazing for the art fair, no matter what. But as she turned back to her canvas, Kiyana couldn't help but wonder – what truth was hidden behind her art? And who was trying to tell her?

Meanwhile, Riyan's low, cautious tone over the phone betrayed a hint of knowledge, but the truth itself remained hidden behind his carefully chosen words.

From the breeze that carries her world...

Dear Moonlight,

I had a really strange dream last night. It wasn't like any dream I've had before. I didn't see much, but I heard my name. It was whispered, soft, but it felt... so familiar. Like someone I knew really well was calling me. It left me with this weird feeling, like something important was just out of reach.

These dreams keep happening, and I feel like they're trying to tell me something. I'm trying to figure out my past, but it's like looking at a blurry picture. Mom and Dad are great, but I know they're holding back some things. I remember bits and pieces of being a kid – fun times, birthday parties, trips with the family. But there are these big empty spaces, like pages ripped out of a book.

Riyan's been acting kind of weird lately. He says we need to talk about my past, but I'm just not ready yet. I told him I need to focus on the art fair, and he said he'd wait. But I know he's going to tell me something soon.

My art is my favorite place to be. When I paint, I feel like I can breathe. It's like I'm connecting with a part of myself I don't totally get. My new painting, "Echoes in the Night," is about those dreams and feelings I have.

After the art fair, I'll be ready to hear what Riyan has to say. I'll find out what's going on, no matter how hard it might be.

Until then, I'll keep painting and trying to figure things out.

Yours truly,
Kiyana

Aarav...

arav's eyes narrowed as he framed the shot, the camera's viewfinder his window to the world. He clicked the shutter, capturing the city's vibrant chaos. Photography was his escape, his desire

As he walked through the bustling streets, Aarav's gaze lingered on the people around him. He saw stories in every face, every gesture. His lens captured the beauty, the pain, and the resilience.

But Aarav's own story was one of the scars. His mother had passed away when he was just a child, leaving him with a void that could never be filled. His father, a critic, had raised him with an iron fist, teaching him to rely only on himself. *Love was a luxury Aarav couldn't afford.* He'd learned to shield himself from emotions, to focus on the practical, the tangible.

As he turned a corner, the hospital loomed before him. Aarav's heart flipped a little. He'd been visiting the hospital for months now, ever since his younger sister, Aria, had been admitted. She was the last shred of family he had to hold onto. The hospital's sterile corridors seemed to stretch on forever as Aarav walked, his footsteps echoing off the walls. The doctors' words still lingered in his mind: *"We're doing everything we can, but..."* The unspoken words hung in the air like a challenge.

As he entered Aria's hospital room, his heart twisted, a mix of emotions swirling inside him. Aria lay motionless, her small frame swallowed by the bed. Aarav's eyes locked onto hers, his heart pounding in anticipation. Suddenly, Aria's eyes flickered open, and she smiled weakly. "Hey, bhaiya," she whispered, her voice barely audible.

Aarav's face broke into a smile as he sat beside her. "Hey, aaru. How are you feeling?"Aria's gaze drifted to the camera around his neck. "You've been taking pictures again, haven't you?"Aarav nodded, his eyes never leaving hers. "Yeah, I have. It helps me clear my head."Aria's expression turned serious. "You need to be careful, bhaiya. There are things you don't understand... things that could hurt you."Aarav's brow furrowed in concern. "What are you talking about, Aria?"

But before she could respond, Aarav's phone buzzed, shrill in the silent room. He hesitated, unsure whether to answer. Aria's eyes locked onto his. "Answer it, bhaiya. It might be important."

Aarav's heartbeat hesitated as he took the call. The voice on the other end was unfamiliar, but the words sent a shiver down his spine: "We've been watching you, Aarav. You're getting close to the truth."As he listened, Aarav's gaze drifted to the mysterious letter on his lap he received right before he came to meet Aria. The words danced on the page, but one phrase stood out: *"She's awake."*

Aarav's eyes locked onto Aria's, his heart pounding in anticipation. Was this connected to his sister's condition?

The questions swirled in his mind like a vortex, pulling him deeper into the mystery. Aarav's grip on the camera tightened, his mind racing with possibilities.

As he ended the call, Aria's voice whispered in his ear: "I think things are going to change in your life bhaiya for your good.."

The next day...

Aarav stood outside the ICU, his eyes fixed on the frail figure of his sister, Aria. The sterile white walls and the antiseptic smell transported him to a different time, a different line. Dr Patel, a middle aged man with a kind face, approached him "Aarav, we need to discuss Aria's condition; she requires immediate surgery." He said to Aarav, "The only person who can help us now is him. We need his steady hands and his expertise. We cannot afford to lose any more time."

Aarav's gaze drifted away his mind clouded by the memories he thought were long buried the doctor's words echoed in his mind and suddenly he was back in a different hospital in a different room, standing beside a different bed memories flooded his mind like a dam breaking he remembered the countless nights he had spent by her side holding her frail hand and praying for her recovery. He recalled the fateful day, the sweat dripping from his brow and the weight of responsibility crushing him. The consequences of that day still haunt him; the what-ifs and if-onlys had become his constant companion, a shadow that followed him everywhere.

Aarav's eyes welled up with tears as he struggled to push those memories away; he took a deep breath and composed himself. He replied to the doctor in a firm yet cracked voice," don't forget doctor the steady hand you're talking about he took my love's life away he promised to save her instead he shattered me, my love everything and everyone". In his firm voice he said " I have a very good friend of mine 'Arjun' a renowned specialist in London I'll arrange for aaru to be transferred there he will ensure she receives the best care possible."

As doctor walked away he looked at Aria with concern he rushed to her side taking her hand in his "I'm here,aaru I'll take care of you you'll be fine trust me I promise" Aria said "I know bhaiya I trust you beyond words..."tears streamed down aarav's face as he smiled trying to reassure his sister *but deep within he knew he was still trapped in the prison of his past searching for a way to break free , to heal , and to find solace in the world that seemed to have moved on without him*

....

London calling…

Aarav kept his promise. He was a man of his word, especially when it came to Aria. He wouldn't let his past dictate his sister's future. He arranged for her transfer to London, his heart heavy but his resolve strong. He knew he was doing the right thing.

As their plane touched down at Heathrow, a sense of quiet determination settled over Aarav. He was here for Aria, and he would make sure she got the best care possible.

Dr. Arjun, Aarav's best friend, was waiting for them at the hospital. They had been friends for years, their bond forged in shared experiences and mutual respect. Arjun was more than a friend; he was like family to Aarav.

"Aarav, it's good to see you," Arjun said, his voice warm and reassuring. He gave Aarav a firm handshake, a silent acknowledgment of the difficult journey they were about to embark on. "And Aria, you're in good hands here."

Aria smiled, her eyes filled with gratitude. "Thank you, Arjun," she said.

Aarav and Arjun shared a look, a silent conversation passing between them. They understood each other without needing many words.

Aria's treatment started immediately, and within a few days, she was showing remarkable improvement. "I told you, bhaiya," she said, her voice filled with playful confidence, "Arjun is the best!"

Aarav chuckled, relief washing over him. "Yes, he is," he agreed, patting Arjun's shoulder. "Thank you, Arjun. I don't know what I'd do without you."

"We're family, Aarav," Arjun said, his voice sincere. "We look out for each other."

One afternoon, as they sat in Arjun's office, discussing Aria's progress, Aarav frowned. "Arjun, I've been getting some strange messages," he said, his voice low. "Cryptic notes, things that don't make sense."

Arjun raised an eyebrow. "Strange messages? What kind of messages?"

"I don't know," Aarav said, his voice troubled. "They seem… personal. Like someone knows me."

Arjun smiled, a knowing glint in his eyes. "Maybe someone is trying to help you," he said, winking.

Aarav's expression turned serious. "This isn't funny, Arjun," he said. "You know things have changed. Things are different now."

"I know," Arjun said, his voice softening. "And I think I'm already in a bit of danger helping you with something… suspicious."

Arjun's subtle hints and cryptic messages had been puzzling Aarav for weeks, but now the truth dawned on him. His friend had been secretly working to bring him and Kiyana together, carefully planting clues to keep Aarav's rival from interfering. It was a delicate balancing act, driven by Arjun's loyalty and determination to protect Aarav's heart. With each mysterious text and whispered warning, Arjun had been quietly guiding Aarav toward a reunion that would heal old wounds and rekindle a love that never truly faded.

He paused, then added casually, "You know, Kiyana is perfectly fine."

Aarav's breath hitched. The name, "Kiyana," felt like a punch to the gut, a surge of emotions he thought he had buried long ago. His eyes widened, a flicker of hope and pain flashing across his face. "Kiyana?" he echoed, his voice barely a whisper. "She's alive and …she is in London?" his eyes welled up.

As the name "Kiyana" whispered through the air, Aarav's mind was catapulted back to a time when love was pure, and hearts were whole. Memories he thought were long buried began to resurface, like whispers from a past life. Every moment, every laugh, every tear he'd shared with Kiyana came flooding back, and Aarav's heart swelled with a mix of emotions.

He'd never given up on her, never stopped loving her, even when the world had convinced him that she was gone and he told him to move on. But he'd resigned himself to a life without her, a life where the ache of her absence had become a familiar companion. Yet, the spark of hope had never fully extinguished, and now, with Arjun's cryptic words, that spark had burst into a flame.

But one thing was certain: Aarav's heart still belonged to Kiyana, and if there was even a glimmer of a chance to rekindle what they'd once shared, he was willing to take the leap. The question was, would she still be his, or had life taken her down a different path?

As the questions swirled in his mind, Aarav felt the familiar tug of longing, a longing that had haunted him for years. He took a deep breath, steeling himself for what was to come, knowing that the journey ahead would be fraught with uncertainty, but driven by the hope of reuniting with the love of his life.

Aria, who had been listening quietly, smiled softly. "Yes, bhaiya," she said. "Arjun helped me. I knew you'd listen to him."

Aarav looked at Arjun, his mind reeling with conflicting emotions. "Why didn't you tell me?"

he asked, his voice strained.

"Because," Arjun said, his voice gentle, "sometimes, you need to find things out for yourself. Besides, I think the art fair might be a good place to start."

"Is there a reason you keep mentioning the art fair, Arjun?" Aarav asked, his voice laced with suspicion. "Is this related to those… suggestions you've been making?"

Arjun's smile faltered slightly, but he quickly recovered. "Just a coincidence," he said, his voice a little too casual. "But it might be a good opportunity for you to… see something different. Maybe something that will help you let go of old burdens."

Before the art fair...

Kiyana fidgeted in her seat, her eyes darting towards the window as the warm sunlight streaming in highlighted her anxiety. She was at Dr. Arjun's clinic for her regular check-up, a routine that still made her feel a little uneasy. The clinic's sterile smell, a stark contrast to the vibrant colors of her upcoming art fair, only added to her nerves. Riyan, sensing her unease, placed a reassuring hand on her shoulder. His calm demeanor was a balm to her frazzled nerves.

Across the city, in a newly furnished apartment, Aarav and Aria were settling into their temporary London home. Aria was doing remarkably well, her health steadily improving under Dr. Arjun's care. The apartment, though unfamiliar, offered a sense of peace, a quiet haven in the bustling city. Aarav, however, couldn't shake the feeling that something significant was about to happen. He felt like the universe was rearranging itself, aligning events in a way that was both mysterious and inevitable.

They say the universe has a way of aligning everything for us, of bringing people and events together at just the right moment. And as Kiyana waited for her appointment and

Aarav unpacked in his new apartment, unseen forces were already at work, weaving their destinies together.

As Dr. Arjun began to speak, Riyan's gaze narrowed slightly, his eyes locked onto the doctor's. There was something about the way Dr. Arjun's warm, honey-brown eyes crinkled at the corners as he smiled at Kiyana that didn't sit right with Riyan. He couldn't quite put his finger on it, but his instincts were screaming at him to be cautious.

Dr. Arjun, meanwhile, thought to himself, *Riyan is always aware of the consequences. He is always two steps ahead. He also thought, Once Aarav is a little free from his sister's treatment, I am sure he will be the most impossible task to handle for his rival. He knew Aarav was someone who wouldn't just sit back. He was a man who would act. And I know I am already in a bit of danger by helping him with something really special yet suspicious*

"Don't worry, Kiyana," Dr. Arjun said, his voice soothing, "Everything looks good. You're perfectly healthy."

Relief washed over Kiyana, a genuine smile gracing her lips. "Thank you, Doctor. I was a bit anxious."

As they stepped out of the clinic, the warm sunlight and gentle breeze enveloped them, but Kiyana's demeanor remained shrouded in concern. Her usual carefree spirit had given way to a brooding intensity, her eyes clouded with a mix of fear and uncertainty.

Riyan noticed the change in her and his expression turned sympathetic. "Hey Ki, I've been watching you, and I have to say, you're blooming like a flower every day. Your health is on the mend, and as far as I can see, you're doing great." Riyan's voice was a soothing melody, low and gentle, with a hint of warmth that made her pulse flutter. He paused, his eyes locking onto hers with an intensity that made her feel seen. "But I know you, Ki. I know when something's eating away at you. So, tell me, is there anything bothering you? Anything you want to talk about?"

Kiyana hesitated, her eyes darting around the crowded street before focusing on Riyan's. "You remember !? I told you that I've been getting some... strange messages lately," she said, her voice barely above a whisper.

Riyan's frown deepened, a slight crease forming between his brows. "Yes of course, but I thought they were just a prank or something..," he pressed, his eyes locked onto hers.

Kiyana's gaze dropped, her voice taking on a hesitant tone. "No, I really don't think it was a prank. They are something more than that, you know. Just... cryptic things. Hints, mostly. They feel... important somehow." Her eyes narrowed, as if she was trying to decipher the meaning behind the messages.

Riyan's expression turned skeptical, a hint of amusement dancing in his eyes. "I don't know, Ki. Maybe it's actually just a prank and might be you're overthinking." He shrugged, his eyes sweeping the street, taking in the sights and sounds of the bustling city.

But Kiyana's smile faltered, her eyes clouding over with concern. "I don't think so," she said, her voice firm. "They feel... personal." Her voice trailed off, leaving Riyan to wonder what she meant.

Riyan's gaze snapped back to hers, his expression softening. He sensed her unease and placed a hand on her shoulder, his touch warm and reassuring. But as his hand lingered, Kiyana felt a shiver run down her spine. Riyan's touch, usually comforting, felt intrusive now, as if he was crossing a boundary she hadn't explicitly set.

"Don't worry, Ki," " Riyan said, his voice low and soothing. "I'll look into it. We'll figure out who's behind these messages and put a stop to it." His eyes locked onto hers, filled with a determination that made Kiyana feel both grateful and uneasy.

Riyan…

Riyan's office was a stark contrast to the warmth of his conversation with Kiyana. The walls were a cold, sterile white, and the furniture was all sharp angles and hard surfaces. The only color in the room came from the harsh fluorescent lights that buzzed overhead, casting an unnatural glow on everything. Even the plants in the corners looked wilted and sickly.

Riyan's employees were all too aware of his reputation. He was a man who demanded results, and he wasn't afraid to fire anyone who didn't meet his expectations. As a result, everyone tiptoed around him, afraid to make even the smallest mistake. Rachel, his assistant, knew this better than anyone. She had seen him fire people for far less than this.

"Sir, we have an important meeting scheduled with the investors today," she said, her voice barely a whisper. "It's a multimillion-dollar deal, and they're not willing to reschedule."

Riyan didn't even look up from his phone. "Cancel it," he said, his voice flat and emotionless.

Rachel's eyes widened. "Sir, I don't think that's wise. This deal could make or break our company."

Riyan finally looked up, his eyes cold and hard. "Nothing is more important than Kiyana right now. You'd do well to remember that, Rachel. Don't repeat this mistake again."

Rachel nodded quickly, her face pale. She knew better than to argue with him. She turned and hurried out of the office, her heart pounding in her chest.

Riyan's focus returned to the text conversation with Kiyana. Her message about needing help with her art pieces had been a welcome distraction from the unease that had been growing inside him.

"Hey, Ki. I'll come by tomorrow and help you with your art pieces. Don't worry, I've got you covered," he replied, his thumbs flying across the keyboard.

Kiyana's response was immediate. "Thanks, Riyan. I really appreciate it."

Riyan's eyes crinkled at the corners as he smiled. He couldn't wait to see her tomorrow.

Meanwhile Riyan was still stuck with the thought of her getting weird messages. His gut told him something was off, and he couldn't shake the feeling that Kiyana might be in danger or there could be some consequences of truth which could destroy him and his very existence that he had built around her.

Later, He had a meeting with his detective friend Marcus his expression was grim as he laid out the information he had gathered.

"Dr. Arjun's been acting suspiciously, Riyan. He's been in contact with some shady characters, and I think he might be involved in something big."

Riyan's eyes narrowed. "Get me everything you can on Dr. Arjun. I want to know what he's hiding."

Marcus nodded and handed Riyan a folder filled with documents and photographs.

As Riyan flipped through the contents, his mind racing with possibilities, he knew he had to take action. He couldn't let Kiyana get hurt.

With a sense of determination, Riyan picked up his phone and sent a text message to Dr. Arjun.

"Meet me at McGillicuddy's at 8 pm. Come alone."

The message was simple, but the underlying threat was clear. Riyan was watching, and he wouldn't hesitate to take action if necessary.

Later that evening, Riyan found himself in a dimly lit bar, the scent of old wood and stale beer heavy in the air. He sat opposite Dr. Arjun, the clinking of ice in glasses the only sound in the otherwise hushed atmosphere. Dr. Arjun, oblivious to the danger that lurked in Riyan's eyes, sipped his drink, his gaze drawn to the flickering neon sign outside, casting an queer glow on the street.

"I've been observing you, Doctor," Riyan began, his voice a silken whisper, his gaze unwavering. "And I've noticed your... interest in Kiyana's life and somehow I would say you're interested in helping your best friend ain't you !?."he smirks

Dr. Arjun chuckled, a hint of sadness in his eyes. "She's a remarkable young woman. It's a pleasure to know her. But she's… lost. Confused. And there's someone out there who loves her deeply."

Riyan's eyes narrowed, a predatory glint reflecting in the dim light. "Who?"

Dr. Arjun hesitated, then said, "Someone who would do anything for her. Someone who deserves her love."

A wave of cold dread washed over Riyan. He knew who Dr. Arjun was referring to: Aarav. This confirmed his suspicions. Dr. Arjun, as Aarav's best friend, was trying to subtly guide Kiyana towards the truth, towards the man she truly belonged with.

"I appreciate your concern, Doctor," Riyan said, his voice deceptively calm, his hand casually resting on the edge of the table, his fingers tracing the grain of the wood. "But Kiyana's happiness is my concern too."

Dr. Arjun, sensing the shift in the atmosphere, frowned. "What are you implying?"

Riyan let out a low, humorless laugh, the sound echoing in the hushed bar. "That you're trying to meddle in her life. To manipulate her feelings."

Dr. Arjun scoffed, "That's absurd! I'm only trying to help her and guide her to the right path. She deserves better than a love shrouded in darkness and deceit. Beyond the boy who wears a devil's mask, she needs someone who'll love her for who she truly is."

Riyan: (smirking) "And who might that someone be, Doctor?"

Doctor Arjun: "Someone who'll cherish and protect her, not manipulate and control her. You know what they say, fate cannot fail. When he finds out about Kiyana, you won't be able to stop him. Mark my words."

"Oh, poor Doctor Arjun. Do you think you can do that? No, you cannot. Even fate couldn't. Who the hell are you to think you can change her destiny?"

He leaned forward, his gaze intense, a chilling smile playing on his lips. "I wouldn't want anything to happen to you, Doctor. *Accidents do happen, you know. In the most unexpected ways.*" His hand, now resting on Dr. Arjun's arm, tightened slightly, sending a jolt of fear through the doctor. Dr. Arjun, his face pale, watched Riyan leave, the chilling words echoing in his mind, the weight of the unspoken threat heavy upon him.

Riyan wasn't born a villain. Kiyana was his turning point. For her, he'd rewrite the rules of right and wrong. He would blur any line,cross any boundary. His need to have her in his life was a fire that consumed everything in his path.

Kiyana, meanwhile, was preparing for her art fair, excitement bubbling within her as she carefully arranged her paintings. The bright colors seemed to mock the growing unease that had begun to creep into her mind. The cryptic messages, Riyan's secretive behavior, and the lingering darkness in his eyes all contributed to a nagging sense of unease. She tried to dismiss it as overthinking, focusing on the beauty of her artwork, but a shiver ran down her spine, a chilling reminder that something was amiss.

The art fair…

The calendar flipped to the 16th of September, and a cool, chilling air swept through the city, a gentle prelude to the day's unfolding drama. The sky, a canvas of soft pinks, hinted at a day touched by magic. Riyan, his devilish mask slipping, had spent the morning helping Kiyana transport her art pieces to the fair. Little did she know, the shadows he cast were lengthening. His attention was diverted by a call from his detective, Marcus. He was deeply engrossed. His voice, laced with urgency, warned him to be vigilant, "Aarav might be there, be cautious."

Meanwhile, Aarav and Aria, their bond, a fortress of sibling love, were also making their way to the art fair. Aria, still recovering, was under Aarav's watchful eye. "Bhaiya, don't worry," she reassured him, "I told you, your life is going to change in a good way, and this is the sign."

As Aarav approached the art fair, a strange shift occurred. The gentle breeze turned into a sudden gust, and the pinkish sky deepened, as if fate itself were drawing attention to the moment. It was as if the universe whispered, *This is the place, this is the time. The air was charged with love as if fate was about to reveal a secret*

Aarav spotted Kiyana from across the bustling fair. His heart skipped a beat. Five years. That's how long Aarav had carried a hollow space inside him, a constant reminder of Kiyana's missing laughter. Like old photos left in the sun, memories of their time together had grown faint, but the sadness never went away. Then, through the lively crowd of the fair, a burst of light caught his eye, and his heart twisted in his chest. Kiyana. She was there, glowing, her hands moving with a powerful energy as she painted.

Aarav's breath hitched as he moved closer, his eyes fixed on hers. Tears welled up as he took in the sight of her. He'd believed he'd never see her again, never hear her laugh, never feel her close. But she was real, alive, and painting with a beauty that made his heart race.

The noise of the fair faded, and it felt like only they existed, in a moment filled with all the things that could have been. Aarav's heart pounded as he took another step, his whole being reaching for hers. He'd pictured this moment so many times, but nothing could have prepared him for the flood of feelings that threatened to overwhelm him.

She was alive. Painting. Breathing. *That simple fact washed over him like a wave, pushing away the sadness, the hurt, and the longing of five years. Aarav felt like he could finally breathe again, like he'd found a missing part of himself, a part he thought was lost forever.*

He watched her, lost in the beauty of her art, and thought to himself, *"To watch someone vanish into their passion, It's like catching starlight. A rare and beautiful thing, like seeing their heart shine, a glimpse of the magic they hold inside."*

Aarav took a deep breath and walked towards her, his heart pounding a little too fast. Kiyana, surrounded by her art, felt someone approaching. She turned, her eyes meeting him. "Hey, how can I help you? Are you here to look at the paintings?"

It was as if the very fabric of their history had been torn apart, leaving him with a gaping hole where his heart once was.The realization crept over him like a slow-moving shadow, darkening every memory, every laugh, every whispered promise. He was a ghost from her past,a forgotten chapter in the story of her life.

Aarav's heart was exploding with emotions.*"It was a moment that froze time, a moment that shattered my world. I stood before her, my heart racing with excitement, expecting the familiar sparkle in her eyes, the warm smile that would light up her face. But instead, I was met with a blank stare, a puzzled expression that made my heart sink. In that instant, I knew something was terribly wrong. She didn't recognize me.*

Tears pricked at the corners of my eyes as I whispered her name, hoping against hope that something would spark, something would bring back the memories we'd shared. But there was only silence.

I thought of all the moments we'd shared, all the laughter, all the adventures. I thought of the promises we'd made, the vows we'd whispered to each other. And I realized that it was all gone. Erased.

My heart felt like it was shattering into a million pieces, each one piercing me like a shard of glass. I felt like I was bleeding from the inside out, like my very soul was being torn apart."

Aarav, still reeling from the fact she didn't seem to recognize him, quickly composed himself. "Hi,"he said, trying to keep his voice steady. "I'm a photographer. And I'd really love to take some pictures of your work. They're amazing."

"Thank you so much!" Kiyana smiled, a warm, genuine smile that made his heart skip a beat. "Yeah, sure, go ahead."

"Amazing?" Aarav said, adding a touch of playful sarcasm. " That's an understatement. They're so good, they're practically stealing my ability to see any other art."

Kiyana laughed, her eyes sparkling. "Oh, I'm sorry, are my paintings too bright for your sophisticated photographer eyes?"

"Only when they're reflecting your brilliance," Aarav quipped, a playful smirk on his face.

" Oh wow, someone's a poet now," Kiyana replied, her tone light and teasing.

"Aarav," he said, extending his hand. "I'm Aarav."

As Kiyana took his hand, a strange feeling washed over her. 'Aarav,' she repeated softly, her brow furrowed slightly. *The name felt...familiar, like a half-remembered melody.* It was like a whisper in the back of her mind, a feeling she couldn't quite place. And then she looked at him.

He had warm, brown eyes, the kind that seemed to hold a thousand stories, and a slightly rugged look that was undeniably attractive. His dark hair was a bit messy, like he'd just run his hands through it, and there was a hint of stubble that made him look approachable, but also a little mysterious. As he moved, she saw the way his broad shoulders filled out his shirt, and a strange sense of familiarity washed over her.

A flash of memory flickered in her mind—a camera clicking, brown eyes focused, a voice saying, *"Perfect."* But it was gone as quickly as it came.

"That name... it sounds familiar. Have we met before?" she asked, her voice a little shaky.

"Maybe in a past life?" Aarav joked, trying to keep things light. "Or maybe you've just heard about my legendary photography skills?"

Kiyana chuckled, but her eyes held a hint of confusion. "Maybe," she said, still trying to shake the feeling. "I've had some memory gaps lately, so I might be imagining things."

Their conversation flowed, a mix of emotions and witty banter, the air crackling with an unspoken tension. It was their first encounter in five years, a strange blend of newness and something else, something deeper.

Suddenly, Aarav saw Riyan approaching. He knew Riyan's hidden darkness, the part others didn't see. He knew what Riyan was capable of. With a quick excuse, Aarav slipped away, not out of fear, but out of a fierce determination to protect Kiyana. *"I'll do whatever it takes to make you remember,"* he vowed to himself, his eyes filled with a newfound resolve.

From the wind that Whispers his name..

Dear starlight,

Today, the universe conspired to bring me back to life. As I locked eyes with her, the fragments of my shattered heart began to mend. Five years of longing, of aching, of dying a little every day, all dissolved into nothingness. She was alive, and that was all that mattered.

But as I gazed deeper into her eyes, I saw a stranger staring back at me. The memories we had crafted together, the laughter we had shared, the tears we had cried – all gone. Erased from her mind like a painting wiped clean from a canvas.

I felt like I was holding onto a fading light, desperately trying to keep it from extinguishing. But with every passing moment, it slipped further away, leaving me in darkness.

My soul wept at the realization. Riyan, that master manipulator, had woven a web of deceit around her. He had stolen her memories, her identity, and her love. But I vowed to reclaim it all for her. I would be her memory, her guiding light, her shelter from the storm.

As I watched her, I felt the fire of determination ignite within me. I would move heaven and earth to bring her memories back. I'll fight for every lost memory, every stolen moment, I'll break down the walls he's built around her to give her every ounce of happiness she deserves, to give her the world where she truly belongs.

Dr. Arjun's cryptic messages had been my lifeline, my beacon of hope. He knew the danger Riyan posed, still he had put himself into danger for helping me. The reason he is not just my friend but my brother. Aria's improving health was my strength. With Arjun and Aria by my side I know we can overcome anything.

I know Riyan suspects I'm back. He'll be waiting, ready to play the villain once more. But this time,

 our story would unfold differently. I would ensure that our love wins over the forces of darkness. This time, I will make it right, no matter the cost. History won't repeat itself. It will be rewritten, and it will be ours.

 Yours truly,
Aarav

Kiyana …

Kiyana sat on her bed, phone pressed tightly to her ear. "Mom," she said, her voice a little wobbly, "the art fair was… actually really good. I sold some paintings. But it just made me miss you guys so much."

"Oh, sweetie," her mom's voice came through the phone, warm like a hug. "I miss you too, Kiya. And I'm so, so proud of you. You're doing what you love, making beautiful things."

"It's just not the same without you," Kiyana sighed, looking out the window. "And sometimes… It feels like there's something important I am missing . Like a part of me is gone."

"I know, honey," her mom said gently. "It's been a long time. Five years is a long time to live with missing memories."

"Riyan says they'll come back," Kiyana said, her voice full of doubt.

"Riyan's been there for you through everything," her mom said, her voice strong but kind. "Trust him, Kiya. He wants what's best for you. It's time, sweetie. It's time to find out what happened that night."

Kiyana's heart started to race. "I'm scared, Mom."

"It's okay to be scared," her mom reassured her. "But you're strong, Kiya. You can handle this."

"Yeah, you're right. I'll deal with it," Kiyana said, taking a deep breath. "Thank you, Mom. Talking to you always makes me feel better. Love you."

"Love you too, Kiya. Take care," her mom replied.

From the breeze that carries her world

Dear moonlight,

Today, I talked to Mom. It always makes me feel a little better, even though I still feel lost. She told me to trust Riyan, that he's been there for me. I know she's right, he has. But something feels off. Like there's a secret he's keeping. And she said it's time to know what happened to me. Five years... that's a long time to forget so much. I'm scared to know, but I'm also tired of feeling like I'm living someone else's life. What if I don't like who I was before? What if the truth is too painful? I wish I could just remember everything, all at once. But I guess that's not how it works. Riyan's coming over later to talk. I hope he tells me the truth. I need to know.

Also, something strange happened at the art fair. A man came to look at my paintings. He said he was a photographer. He had warm brown eyes that felt really familiar, and his name was Aarav. We talked for a bit, and he was funny and kind. But then, just like that, he was gone. It was like he disappeared. I don't know why, but I feel like I know him from somewhere. It's so weird. Maybe it's just my imagination playing tricks on me.

I guess tomorrow will bring answers and maybe I'll finally face it ..

Yours truly,
Kiyana

The next day: Riyan …

Riyan slammed his fist on the desk, the scattered photos of Aarav and Kiyana. He'd been so sure he'd covered his tracks, but Aarav was back, bold and better this time, right there at the art fair. He'd missed him. A cold fury settled in Riyan's gut. He'd been so focused on keeping Kiyana in his carefully constructed world, he'd let his guard down. That was a mistake he wouldn't make again.

"Marcus," he growled, his voice tight, "those documents better be perfect. Aarav's back, and he's watching. We can't afford any slip-ups."

"They're almost ready," Marcus said, his voice a little shaky. "Just finalizing the photo edits. We'll make it look like…"

"Like the truth," Riyan interrupted, his eyes hard. "A truth Kiyana will believe." He needed to rewrite her past, he needed to control the narrative, to steer Kiyana away from the real truth. He'd create a version of her past, one that kept her firmly in his grasp.

A few days later, Riyan called Kiyana, forcing a casual tone. "Hey, Ki, how did the art fair go?"

"It was alright," Kiyana said, her voice a little distant. "A few sales. It was good to see people appreciate the work."

"That's fantastic," Riyan said, his mind racing. "Listen, can I drop by your studio later? I want to talk about something important."

"Sure, Riyan," she said. "Come whenever."

Later, as Riyan walked into Kiyana's studio, he forced a smile. The smell of paint and canvas, usually so comforting, now felt suffocating. He had to be convincing. "Nice place," he said, scanning the room. "You've really made it your own."

"Thanks," Kiyana said, offering him a seat. "So, what did you want to talk about?"

"Just checking in," he said, feigning concern. "How are you feeling? Any more of those dreams?"

"A few," she admitted, her brow furrowed. "They're still confusing."

Riyan sighed, a long, drawn-out sound that spoke of weariness and hidden burdens. "Ki," he began, his voice soft, almost hesitant, "it's been five years. Five years of you living in this...limbo. Five years of me watching you struggle with fragments and shadows. Don't you think it's time we tried to piece things together?"

A wave of conflicting emotions washed over Kiyana. Relief, fear, and a desperate yearning for the truth warred within her. "But… I don't understand. You've always said it would come back naturally. That forcing it would only make things worse."

"And I still believe that, to an extent," Riyan replied, his voice laced with a strange urgency. "But sometimes, Ki, a gentle push is needed. Sometimes, you need to open a door to let the light in."

He paused, a bit of silence stretching between them. "Your dream… It sounded vivid. Too vivid to be just a random nightmare."

Kiyana shivered, the memory of her dream still sharp and raw. "It felt real," she admitted, her voice trembling. "Like… like I was reliving something."

"Exactly," Riyan said, his voice low and intense. "And that's why we need to talk. We need to explore those fragments, those whispers in the dark. We need to find out what happened that night, Ki. For your sake."

A sudden suspicion flickered in Kiyana's mind. "Why now, Riyan? Why are you suddenly so eager to delve into my past?"

Riyan hesitated, a flicker of something unreadable crossing his face. "Because," he said, his voice strained, "I can't bear to see you like this anymore. I can't bear to see you living a half-life, haunted by ghosts you can't name."

He paused, then added, his voice barely a whisper, "And because… some things need to be said."

Kiyana's heart pounded in her chest, a frantic rhythm against her ribs. She could sense Riyan holding back, hiding something behind his carefully constructed facade. "What things?" she asked, her voice sharp with suspicion.

"Things about your past, Ki," Riyan replied, his voice laced with a hint of sadness. "Things about… the accident."

"What about it?" she asked, her voice barely audible.

"There are things you don't know, Ki," Riyan said, his voice low and mysterious. "Things that might… change everything."

He was silent for a moment, then added, his voice laced with a hint of warning, "But are you sure you want to know?"

Kiyana's breath caught in her throat. She was terrified, yet irresistibly drawn to the truth. "Yes," she whispered, her voice filled with a desperate longing. "Tell me everything."

Riyan sighed, a sound of resignation and sorrow. "Alright, Ki," he said, his voice heavy with unspoken words. *He knew he had her attention, and he was ready to weave his web of lies.*

…….

The web of lies…

Kiyana stared at Riyan, her heart pounding. "We were getting married?" she whispered, her voice shaking. "That's… impossible."

She'd always seen Riyan as her best friend, the one person she could always count on. But a fiancé? That felt completely wrong, like a puzzle piece forced into the wrong place.

Riyan sighed, pulling out a folder. He slid it across the table. Inside were photos. Kiyana's breath caught in her throat.

There she was, in a beautiful Indian wedding dress, a shimmering saree of red and gold. She looked radiant, but also… like a stranger. In some photos, she was laughing with Riyan, who was dressed as a groom. In others, she was alone, her expression thoughtful, almost sad.

"This… this can't be real," she murmured, her head spinning.

Her memory was a blank slate, but these photos felt like a lie. Riyan was her friend, not her fiancé.

"Ki," Riyan said, his voice soft, "I know this is a lot to take in. But it's the truth. We were going to get married. And then... the accident happened."

"No," Kiyana said, her voice firm despite her confusion. "You're my friend, Riyan. Just my friend."

"I know it's hard to believe," Riyan said gently. "But look at the photos, Ki. They don't lie. We were happy. We were in love."

Kiyana stared at the photos again, searching for a spark of recognition, a flicker of memory. But there was nothing. Just a deep, unsettling emptiness.

"Riyan," she said, her voice trembling, "I don't remember any of this."

"I know, Ki," he said, his voice filled with a strange sadness. "And I'm so sorry. I wish I could take away your pain. I wish I could give you back your memories."

He paused, then added, "I'll never force you to remember anything you're not ready for. I'll never rush us. I know you're still not prepared to accept the truth, but never mind, you can take your time and trust me. We'll be fine soon. I guess it was high time you needed to know the truth. So here you go."

Kiyana felt a wave of confusion wash over her. Riyan's words were kind, but something in his tone felt... off. Like he was trying too hard to convince her.

She remembered the art fair, the man named Aarav, the strange pull she felt towards him. Now this? It didn't add up.

A flicker of suspicion sparked in her mind. Why was Riyan telling her this now? Why, after five years of silence?

She remembered his hesitation, the way he seemed to choose his words carefully. It was like he was carrying a heavy burden, a secret he was afraid to reveal.

She had a feeling it was more than just her memories that were lost. There was something else, something hidden beneath the surface, something Riyan wasn't telling her.

She looked at the photos again, at her smiling face, at Riyan's gentle gaze. But this time, she saw something else: a hint of sadness in Riyan's eyes, a shadow of guilt. She knew, deep down, that there was more to the story. And she was determined to find out the truth, no matter how painful it might be.

Kiyana's final decision...

Kiyana sat amidst a sea of faded photographs, each one a tiny, fractured memory. *"Marry Riyan,"* her mother's voice echoed in her mind, a gentle yet firm command. *"He'll take care of you, Kiyana. He's a good man."*

Kiyana's fingers traced the outline of a childhood picture, her and Riyan, beaming with innocent smiles. "We were kids," she whispered, the memory feeling distant, almost dreamlike. But as she looked closer, she remembered the way Riyan looked at her now – an intensity that made her skin prickle, a possessiveness that felt unsettling.

"He looks at me like... like I'm a precious prize," she murmured, a shiver running down her spine.

Her mother's words echoed: *"Riyan loves you, Kiyana. He'll build you a secure future."* Kiyana wondered, " But is that enough ?"

That evening, Kiyana spoke to her mother. "Maa, why are you so sure about Riyan?"

"Kiyana, Riyan will take care of you for the rest of your life. He loves you, he is safe." her mother replied.

"But what if I don't love him?" Kiyana asked.

"Love grows, Kiya," her mother replied. "Sometimes, shelter from life's storms is more important than the thrill of passion. You deserve a haven, a place to call home."

Kiyana's parents had been led to believe that Aarav was the one who had ruined their daughter's life. They thought the accident that had taken Kiyana's memories was his fault, a reckless mistake that had forever changed their family's path.

Her mother, fearful of risking Kiyana's life again, had made the decision to keep her away from Aarav. And when Riyan had presented himself as the perfect suitor, her mother had trusted him, trusted that he would keep Kiyana safe.

"Riyan will take care of her," her mother had thought. *"He'll protect her from harm."* Little did she know, Riyan's intentions were far from pure.

Despite her reservations, her mother had always reassured her, "Riyan loves you, Kiya. He'll make you happy." And as she looked at the pictures, she began to wonder if her mother was right. Maybe Riyan was the one for her. Maybe he could make her happy.

As the hours ticked by, her thoughts swirled with memories, both old and new. She thought about the way Riyan made her laugh, the way he listened to her when she needed someone to talk to. And she thought about the documents, the ones with her name and his surname, the ones that promised a future together.

Finally, after what felt like an eternity, she made her decision. She would marry Riyan. She would take a chance on him, on their love, and on their future together.

With a sense of resolve, she met Riyan at the agreed-upon spot. As she looked into his eyes, she saw a flicker of happiness, of excitement.

"I've thought about it, Riyan," she said, her voice barely above a whisper. "I'll marry you."

Riyan's face lit up with a radiant smile. He took her hands, his grip a little too firm. "Ki, You've made me the happiest man alive!", and he swept her into his arms, holding her close.

"I promise you, Ki," he whispered into her ear, "I'll never force you to do anything you don't want to do. You know that, right?"

Kiyana nodded, feeling a wave of emotion wash over her. She knew that Riyan truly loved her, and that thought filled her with a sense of peace.

But as Riyan pulled back to look at her, Kiyana caught a glimpse of something else in his eyes, something that made her heart skip a beat. A flicker of his devilish side, a glimmer of the intensity that had always made her skin prickle.

"I'll make sure you never regret this decision, Kiyana," Riyan said, his voice low and husky. "I'll make sure you're happy, no matter what it takes."

Kiyana felt a shiver run down her spine as she looked into Riyan's eyes.

She trusted him, she knew that much. But love? That was a different story altogether. She couldn't quite put her finger on it, but there was something about Riyan that drew her in, something that made her feel safe, yet uncertain, all at once.

"There's something I need to tell you," Kiyana said, pulling back to look at Riyan. "I've been selected for this nine-day event, where artists from all over the country come together to paint and enjoy nature."

Riyan's eyes sparkled with interest. "That sounds amazing. What's it called?"

"It's called the 'Artists' Retreat'," Kiyana replied. "And I was thinking... after the event, I'll marry you."

Riyan's face lit up with joy, and he pulled her close again.

"I'll wait for you," he whispered. "Forever, if that's what it takes."

As Kiyana lay in bed, she stared at the ceiling, her mind swirling with doubts. " Is this love?" she wondered. "Or just... a gilded cage?"

Life is a journey of choices, and sometimes, the safest path isn't always the happiest one. Kiyana's decision is made, but the true test of her heart is yet to come. Will she find happiness in the security Riyan offers, or will she yearn for something more? Only time will tell.

From the breeze that carries her world

Dear Moonlight,

I feel like I'm drowning in a sea of uncertainty. Mom wants me to marry Riyan, but my heart is filled with doubts. I've known Riyan since childhood, but lately, I've started to notice the subtle changes in his behavior. The way he looks at me, the way he smiles… it's all so intense, so overwhelming.

I've been thinking about our past, about the memories we've shared. Riyan's always been there for me, supporting me, loving me. But is that enough? Can I really spend the rest of my life with him?

I feel like I'm torn between two worlds. One world is filled with the familiarity of Riyan's love, the comfort of knowing what to expect. The other world is filled with uncertainty, with the thrill of the unknown.

I've been selected for the Artists' Retreat, and I feel like it's a sign, a chance for me to discover myself, to find my true path. I felt a small flicker of hope. Maybe these nine days will let me breathe. Maybe I can find myself again.But what if I'm just running away from my problems?

I've decided to marry Riyan after the retreat. I know it sounds crazy, but I feel like I need to take this leap of faith. I need to trust that Riyan will be there to catch me, to support me.

Am I making a mistake? Is this really my destiny? I don't know what the future holds. I feel like I'm walking on a tightrope, and one wrong step could send me falling. I hope I'm strong enough. I hope I can find my own happiness. I hope that even in a gilded cage, a little bird can still learn to sing her own song.

Yours truly,
Kiyana

Where destiny awaits…

Riyan couldn't contain his excitement as he paced back and forth in his living room. Kiyana had finally agreed to marry him, and he knew that nothing could stop him now. He had already won.

"Marcus, my friend," Riyan said, turning to his detective, "I think we've got this in the bag. Kiyana's agreed to marry me, and I don't think Aarav can do anything to stop us now."

Marcus nodded in agreement. "Yes, sir. But we did receive some information that Aarav might be attending the Artists' Retreat, the nine-day event that Kiyana's participating in."

Riyan's smile faltered for a moment, but he quickly regained his composure. "Don't worry about Aarav, Marcus. I've got a plan to take care of him. I'll make sure he's too distracted to cause any trouble."

Marcus raised an eyebrow. "And how do you plan to do that, sir?"

Riyan's smile turned sinister. "I'll make sure Aria's health takes a turn for the worse. Aarav will be too busy worrying about his sister to cause any trouble."

But little did Riyan know, Arjun was Aria's doctor, and she was under his observation. Arjun had been keeping a close eye on Aria's health, and he would not let Riyan's plans come to fruition.

Meanwhile, Aarav was preparing for the Artists' Retreat, his camera equipment at the ready. He had all faith in the divine power that in those nine days, Kiyana would remember everything she had forgotten.

Arjun had helped Aarav get information about the event, and Aarav was grateful for his friend's support.

"Aarav, you have to be careful," Arjun said, as they parted ways. "Riyan's not going to give up easily."

Aarav nodded, his determination clear. "I won't back down, Arjun. I'll make sure Kiyana remembers the truth."

"Time may have stretched the distance between us, but it hasn't diminished the depth of my devotion. This wait has been a pilgrimage of my heart leading me closer to the love we've yet to rediscover" Aarav said.

He built a little garden of hope in his soul watering it with memories and dreams patiently waiting for it to bloom. The art of waiting is not about passing time but about cultivating patience to let love unfold in its own divine time

With the nine-day event just hours away, Aarav felt a sense of destiny calling. He knew that the next few days would change everything, and he was ready to let fate play its role.

From the wind that Whispers his name

Dear starlight,

I believe love is a story written uniquely by each heart it touches. For some it's a curse while for others it's the reason which makes life worth living. It's like a whirlwind of emotions that can lift you up to the skies or drop you to the depth of the sea. It is a puzzle with pieces that form together in unexpected ways. It's a journey filled with twists and turns just when you think you've figured it out, love surprises you with a new twist a new shade of meaning and we often hold onto it even when it hurts because we're afraid to let go off what once brought us so much of happiness it's like bittersweet melodies that stay in our heart a chapter we cannot seem to close

When my soul ached for her presence, but my heart embraced the beauty of her absence. Not anymore because now every sunrise feels like a step closer, a slow golden promise that my story is yet to be written though the hours tick by, my love for her remains ,a constant heartbeat that refuses to fade.

I'm holding onto hope, like it's a little firefly in my hand. I know we'll find our way back to each other, like flowers turning to the sun. Until then, you're in my heart, always growing.

Yours truly,
Aarav

Aarav: his infinite devotion in love

As Aarav stood there, his eyes locked onto Kiyana's, he felt the universe conspire in his favor. It was as if the stars had aligned, the planets had shifted, and the very fabric of fate had woven their lives together once more.

For Aarav, love wasn't a choice; it was Kiyana's smile, her laughter, and her happiness. It was the memories they'd made, the moments they'd shared, and the forever they'd promised. Five years of searching, five years of longing, five years of living in the shadows of what could have been. Aarav's heart had been a battleground, his soul a warrior fighting for the love they shared.

Aarav's empire was built on the pillars of integrity, honesty, and compassion. Everyone knew that he was a man of his word, a man who stood by his principles, and a man who loved with every fiber of his being. Through the storms of life, through the tests of time, Aarav's love for Kiyana remained unwavering. He never wavered, never faltered, and never let go of the love they shared.

As he gazed at Kiyana, Aarav's heart swelled with emotion. He was a man who believed in the power of love, in the beauty of fate, and in the goodness of the universe. He believed that their love was meant to be, that it was a flame that would burn bright for lifetimes to come. And he was willing to wait, to fight, and to pray for that love to be rekindled.

Aarav's thoughts drifted to the prayers he'd whispered, the promises he'd made, and the vows he'd taken. He'd never loved anyone else, never even looked at another woman, for Kiyana was his first, his only, and his forever. He believed in the beauty of their love, in the magic of their connection, and in the wonder of their story.

As the world around him melted away, Aarav knew that he'd been given a rare gift – a chance to relive, to redo, and to reclaim their love. And he was determined to make the most of it, to cherish every moment, and to love Kiyana with every breath in his body. For Aarav knew that their love was a once-in-a-lifetime chance, a fleeting glimpse of heaven on earth, and a beauty that would haunt him for eternity.

Day: 1

Nancy, the retreat's bubbly host, clapped her hands. "Alright, everyone! Time for the painting challenge! We're pairing you up randomly. Each of you, pick a chit with a number. Your partner will have the same number. Also you will be paired up with this partner for the entire event. Good luck with your partners everyone !"

Aarav reached into the bowl, pulling out a folded slip. "Nine," he announced, his voice a little louder than necessary.

Kiyana unfolded her own chit, her eyes widening slightly. "Nine," she echoed, a mix of surprise and something else flickering in her gaze.

As she approached Aarav he couldn't help but admire her, taking in sight of her. She wore a white dress that seemed to float around her, its delicate fabric shimmering in the light. Her hair was loosely gathered in a bun, with a few soft strands escaping to frame her face. Her eyes sparkled with warmth, shining brightly with a gentle, inner light that made her look truly, breathtakingly beautiful.

"You're Aarav, right?" she asked, her voice cool but curious. "We met at the art fair. You... critiqued my work."

Aarav's cheeks warmed slightly. "Right. And you... defended it fiercely," he replied, a small smile playing on his lips. "It's a small world."

"Too small," Kiyana muttered, but a hint of amusement danced in her eyes.

Nancy's voice cut through the air. "Alright, partners! Your theme is... Love. Pure, unadulterated Love! Let the painting begin!"

Aarav stared at the blank canvas. "Listen, I'm a photographer. I capture moments, not paint them. This is all you."

Kiyana sighed, but a spark of determination lit her eyes. She began sketching a vibrant sunset.

"Isn't that a bit... Predictable ?" Aarav asked, his voice laced with a hint of his old critical tone.

"Your eyes see only flaws," Kiyana retorted, her brush strokes becoming more deliberate.

"That's not going to work," Aarav said, shaking his head. " We need something... deeper." He then described her favourite view. "Paint a dark, starry night. A couple sitting beneath it, lost in each other."

Kiyana raised an eyebrow. "Isn't that also predictable?"

Aarav's smile was enigmatic. "Trust me on this."

Kiyana's eyes narrowed, but she began to paint the scene Aarav had described. As she worked, Aarav watched, his eyes fixed on the canvas.

Love, this is the favourite scene of yours, he thought to himself, a realization that stirred something deep within him.

Aarav, despite his initial reluctance, found himself drawn into the process. He watched as Kiyana's brush brought their shared vision to life, the dark canvas blooming with stars and the soft glow of love.

Finally, their painting was finished. A breathtaking scene of a couple bathed in starlight, their love radiating from the canvas.

Aarav stepped back, his eyes fixed on the canvas. "It's beautiful, Kiyana."

Kiyana's face lit up with a warm smile. "Really?" she asked, her voice tinged with uncertainty.

Aarav nodded, his gaze still on the painting. "Yes, really."

Kiyana's smile deepened, her eyes sparkling with pleasure. "Thank you," she said.

Nancy's voice echoed through the room, gathering everyone's attention. "Ladies and gentlemen, please gather around. We'll be declaring the winners soon."

The room buzzed with excitement as people chatted and speculated about the winners.

Nancy smiled, holding up a sheet of paper. "I am here with the winner's names on the list, and I must say, the competition was fierce."

She paused, scanning the room. "Any guesses, guys?"

Kiyana crossed her fingers, a habit she seemed to have when nervous. Aarav watched her, his heart skipping a beat.

Nancy continued, "And the third prize goes to... number seven!"

The room erupted in applause as the winners made their way to the stage.

Nancy smiled. "And the second prize goes to... number eight!"

Kiyana's eyes sparkled with anticipation, her fingers still crossed.

Nancy paused, building the suspense. "And the first prize goes to... number nine!"

Kiyana erupted in a joyful dance, a pure, uninhibited display of happiness. She threw her arms around Aarav, her laughter ringing out. "We won! We actually won!"

Aarav, slightly stunned, His heart was hammering against his ribs, threatening to stop. He looked at her dancing. He was thinking that she was like a child at that moment and he admired her.

he said, his voice a little playful. "I told you, my idea was perfect."

Kiyana rolled her eyes, but her smile was radiant. "It was your idea, but I made it happen!"

"Yeah, yeah," Aarav agreed, his voice softening. "As you say, Miss Ma'am."

Kiyana blushed, her eyes sparkling. "We really did win," she said, her voice filled with wonder.

"Yeah," Aarav echoed, his gaze lingering on her. *"We did."*

"That day was a success," Aarav thought to himself, a quiet satisfaction settling within.

Years of waiting to see her laugh, to see her happy, had finally paid off. And now, as he gazed at Kiyana's radiant smile, he knew that this was only the beginning.

The next chapter was yet to unfold, but for now, Aarav was content to bask in the warmth of this moment, with Kiyana by his side.

Day: 2

The morning was like a soft, fluffy blanket of fog. Kiyana stepped out of her tent, and the wind gently played with her hair. Aarav, watching from his tent, thought, *"I wish I could be that wind."*

"Good morning, Mr. Critic," Kiyana said, her voice light.

"Good morning, Miss Ma'am," Aarav replied, his eyes taking in the misty mountains. "It's a beautiful morning, isn't it?"

"It is," she agreed, looking around.

"Did you have breakfast?" he asked.

"Not yet. I'm not a breakfast person," she said with a little shrug.

"What about tea?" Aarav asked. "You know, a good, warm cup?"

Kiyana's eyes lit up a bit. "In London, they don't make tea like my mom does. I miss her tea so much."

Aarav, seeing his chance, said, "Well, then, today, let me make you some tea. It would be my privilege." He said it with a playful little flirt.

Kiyana laughed, "You just wished me good morning! Why ruin it already?"

"Haha, very funny! Just wait till you taste my tea," Aarav said, grinning. "You'll be amazed!"

He started making the tea, a classic Indian chai, with spices and everything. Kiyana watched him, and he asked, "You don't know how to cook, do you?"

"Nope," she admitted.

"Oh, wow! I know every Indian dish," Aarav said, stirring the tea. "We could be great life partners, don't you think? You'd watch me cook, and I'd make you different dishes every day."

Kiyana smiled and said, "In your dreams!"

He poured her a cup. "Here's your chai, ma'am. Let me know how it tastes."

She took a sip, and her eyes widened. "Oh my god, Aarav! This is really good! I haven't had tea this good in ages."

Aarav flexed his "cooking muscles" playfully. "I told you!"

"Yeah, yeah, whatever," she said, still smiling.

They talked and laughed, enjoying the warm tea and the cool morning.

Suddenly, Nancy's voice rang out. "Good morning, everyone! Today, you'll each be exploring different places. And the task? Well, that's a surprise! You'll find out soon enough."

Nancy continued, "So, be at the beach sharp at 8:00. Don't be late! You won't want to miss this."

Aarav turned to Kiyana. "Are you ready for this?"

Kiyana's smile was radiant. "Yeah born ready"

She was always up for a challenge.

. . . .

The sun cast its golden rays upon the beach, where Aarav and Kiyana stood, cameras in hand. Their challenge was to capture something that held deep meaning, and they'd been assigned the beach as their location. Aarav clicked away, capturing the sea, sand, and seashells. But somehow, it wasn't coming together

"Aarav, look," Kiyana said, pointing to couples of different ages. "Maybe we should ask them to pose with the beach as a backdrop?"

"That's a great idea!" Aarav agreed.

Aarav approached the teen couple, who were gazing out at the ocean, and cleared his throat to get their attention. "Hey, sorry to interrupt, but I'm Aarav, and I'm part of an event team. We're doing a photography task, and I couldn't help but notice how adorable you two are together."

Aarav continued, "Would you guys mind if I clicked some pictures of you both? It would really help us with our task, and I promise I'll make sure you look amazing!"

The couple exchanged a glance, and then nodded in unison, smiling. "Sure, why not?" the boy said, putting his arm around his girlfriend. "We're happy to help."

Aarav grinned, relieved. "Awesome, thanks so much! Just be yourselves, and I'll do the rest."

"What's love to you?" Aarav asked. They answered it beautifully

"Love is... everything. It's the butterflies in your stomach when you see each other, the late-night conversations that feel like they'll never end, and the silly jokes that only make sense to us. It's finding someone who makes you feel like you can be yourself, without judgment. The little things, like the way she smiles when I make her laugh, or the way she always knows how to make me feel better when I'm down. It's the feeling of being home, even when we're not in the same place. And it's the feeling of having a best friend, a partner, and a soulmate all rolled into one."

"That's beautiful," both of them said they thanked the couple.

Next, they met a young adult couple in their late twenties. After they agreed for photos Kiyana asked this time, "What's love for you?"

"Love is... a choice, a commitment, and a journey. It's the everyday moments, the mundane routines, and the quiet sacrifices that show us what love truly means. It's about growing together, learning from each other's flaws, and embracing the imperfections. Love is vulnerability, trust, and acceptance. It's the feeling of being seen, heard, and understood on a deep, unspoken level. And it's the knowledge that through life's ups and downs, you've got someone who's got your back, no matter what."

They were really amazed by their response and their perspective on love

Aarav: "Hey, thanks so much for letting us take your photos! You two are adorable together."

Kiyana: "And thank you for sharing your thoughts on love. Your perspective was really insightful – it's amazing how love can be both exciting and comforting at the same time."

On a bench overlooking the ocean, an elderly couple sat together, hands clasped, watching the sunset paint the sky with hues of crimson and gold. Their faces, etched with the lines of time, told the story of a lifetime of love, laughter, and adventure. As they reminisced about the years gone by, their eyes sparkled with a deep affection, a flame that had burned bright for decades and showed no signs of fading.

Amazed by their lasting love, Aarav and Kiyana asked in unison, "What's love?"

The old couple smiled. And answered..

"Love is... a lifetime of memories, laughter, and tears. It's the accumulation of every moment, big or small, that we've shared together. It's the comfort of familiarity, the security of knowing each other's quirks, and the joy of still discovering new things about each other."

The gentleman's eyes twinkled as he looked at his partner. "After being together for all these years, I wish I could tell God that in my next lifetime, I want her as my partner again."

The lady's face softened, her eyes shining with tears. "In every lifetime, my love, we'll want each other. We'll find each other, no matter what."

Their hands intertwined, a gentle squeeze conveying a lifetime of devotion. "Love is... forever," they whispered in unison.

Aarav: "Sir, ma'am, I just wanted to thank you for sharing your beautiful love story with us. Your photos turned out lovely!"

Elderly Man: "Thank you, dear. We're glad we could be a part of your task."

Kiyana: "And thank you for your wise words on love. Your lifetime of experience and devotion is truly inspiring – a reminder that love only grows stronger with time."

Elderly Woman: "We've been blessed to have found each other. Thank you for listening to our story."

As Aarav and Kiyana prepared to leave, the elderly couple turned to them with warm smiles. "You know, you two look like a couple," the lady said, her eyes twinkling. "Perfect for each other."

The old man leaned in, his voice barely above a whisper, as he spoke to Aarav. "Your eyes don't lie, young man. I wish you both the best." Aarav's face flushed with a gentle blush as he replied, "Thank you, that means a lot."

Aarav: "So, Kiyana, what do you think love is?"

Kiyana: "Hmm, that's a tough one. Love has a lot of definitions, you see."

Aarav: "Yeah, it is different for everyone. I mean, look at that elderly couple over there. They've been together for decades, and their love is still strong."

Kiyana: "Exactly! And then there are the young couples, like that teen pair we photographed earlier. Their love is fresh and exciting, full of possibilities."

Aarav: "Right? And then there are people like us, who may not be in a romantic relationship, but still experience love in other ways – through friendships, family, or even self-love."

Kiyana: "Absolutely. Love is complex, multifaceted. It can't be defined by just one experience or perspective."

Aarav: "I think that's what makes it so beautiful. Love is a mystery, a journey, a choice... and it's different for every single person."

As the sun began its descent, casting a warm orange glow over the horizon, the group stood together, watching the breathtaking view. Kiyana's thoughts drifted back to the old couple's words, and she felt a strange sensation wash over her. Suddenly, she was hit with a vivid flash of a sunset, herself sitting beside someone. Was that Riyan she wondered..

As the night drew to a close, Kiyana and Aarav's work was met with admiration from their group. Nancy praised them, saying, "You two complete each other and always come up with unique ideas."

After dinner, the whole group went stargazing, lying down on their backs to gaze up at the starry night sky. Kiyana pulled out her journal and began to write, while Aarav lay nearby, watching her with a thoughtful expression.

To himself, Aarav whispered, *"Soon, she'll know the truth… and everything will be fine.I watch her, mesmerized, as she writes in her journal. Her brow furrowed in concentration, her pen moving with a gentle precision. I'm drawn to the intimacy of the moment, feeling like I'm witnessing a private ritual."*

The night air was filled with the sound of gentle rustling leaves and the distant breeze, as the group enjoyed the peacefulness of the moment.

From the breeze that carries her world

Dear Moonlight,

I'm sitting here, surrounded by the soothing sounds of nature, and I can barely believe it's only been two days since this event started. It feels like I've experienced a lifetime of emotions already.

These past 48 hours have been nothing short of magical. From the moment we arrived, everything has felt so... soothing. Like a warm hug on a cold day.

Aarav made me chai this morning, and it was a perfect blend of classic indian chai that my mom used to make for me ! We sat together, watching the sunrise, and I felt this sense of peace wash over me.

And then, the competition! We won a prize, but more than that, we met some incredible people. Everyone has a unique story, a different perspective on love. It's been enlightening, to say the least.

But, I have to admit... Being here has given me pause. I'm supposed to marry Riyan after this event, but being around all these people, hearing their stories... It made me wonder if I'm truly ready for that.

I know Riyan is a great guy, and I care about him deeply, but is it love? I'm not so sure anymore. Being here, experiencing all these emotions... It made me realize that I might be settling for something that isn't truly what I want.

I know this might sound crazy, but I feel like I'm at a crossroads. Do I take the safe route, or do I take a chance on something more?

I don't have the answers yet, but I'm grateful for this time to reflect, to rethink what I truly want.

Until next time,

Yours truly,
Kiyana

I know this might sound crazy, but I feel like I'm at a crossroads. Do I take the safe route, or do I take a chance on something more?

I don't have the answers yet, but I'm grateful for this time to reflect, to rethink what I truly want.

Day: 3

The morning arrived like a gentle whisper, a soft golden light painting the dewy grass and the vibrant flowers that surrounded the artist's retreat. A chorus of birdsong filled the air, a sweet melody that seemed to invite everyone to wake and embrace the day. The aroma of freshly brewed coffee and sizzling breakfast filled the common area, a warm and inviting scent that promised a delicious start. Laughter echoed as everyone shared stories from the previous day.

Nancy, her eyes sparkling with enthusiasm, stood up, a gentle smile on her face. "Alright, everyone," she announced, her voice carrying easily through the cheerful chatter. "Today is a free day. Explore, relax, chat, and enjoy the beautiful nature around us."

Aarav turned to Kiyana, his eyes sparkling with excitement. "Hey, want to join me on a nature walk? I heard there's a beautiful waterfall nearby."

Kiyana's face lit up. "Yeah, sure! I'd love to paint there."

As they strolled through the lush green forest, the sound of birdsong and rustling leaves filled the air. Aarav and

Kiyana chatted effortlessly, discussing everything from art to music to their favorite books.

One of their group mates, Rohan, caught up with them, grinning. "You two are like a match made in heaven! I'd rate your partnership 10/10."

Kiyana playfully rolled her eyes. "Um... I'd rate it a five, honestly."

Aarav looked at Kiyana with a teasing smile. "You

mean out of five, right?"

Kiyana blushed, a soft pink tinting her cheeks, and looked away, trying to hide a smile.

As they reached the waterfall, Kiyana gasped in awe. The sunlight danced through the mist, creating a breathtaking rainbow.

Aarav leaned against a nearby rock, watching Kiyana set up her easel. "So, what do you think? Should we add a dash of magic to this painting?"

Kiyana smiled, her eyes sparkling. "I think that's a great idea."

As they stood by the waterfall, the roar of the rushing water creating a soothing melody, Kiyana's gaze drifted off, lost in thought. She was curious about Aarav, about the mysteries he kept hidden behind his piercing eyes.

"So... are you single?" Kiyana asked, her voice barely above a whisper.

Aarav raised an eyebrow, a playful tone in his voice. "Why? Are you interested in me? I mean, yeah, I can pretend to be single for you."winking at her.

Kiyana laughed, a light, airy sound. "No, silly! I'm committed to someone. I'm going to marry him after this event."

Aarav's expression turned serious, his eyes clouding over with memories. "I loved someone deeply,"he said, his voice low and husky. "And I still love her... but I guess fate had some other plans. It was not meant to be back then."

Kiyana's curiosity was at its peak. "What happened to her?" she asked, her voice soft.

Aarav's eyes seemed to glaze over, his gaze fixed on some distant memory. "It was an accident," he said, his voice barely above a whisper.

Kiyana's eyes widened, and she suddenly spaced out, her gaze fixed on some unseen point. Aarav quickly grabbed her arm, concern etched on his face.

"Kiyana, are you okay?" he asked, his voice urgent.

Kiyana blinked, her eyes refocusing on Aarav's worried face. "I... I had a flashback," she said, her voice shaking. "I think it was from my accident. I've been dealing with memory loss... and sometimes, these flashbacks hit me out of nowhere."

Aarav's expression softened, his eyes filled with empathy. "I'm so sorry, Kiyana," he said, his voice gentle. "Is there anything I can do to help?"

Kiyana took a deep breath, composing herself. "No, I'm fine. Just... just give me a minute."

Aarav nodded, his eyes never leaving hers. After a moment, Kiyana continued, her voice stronger now.

"I've been trying to piece together my past," she said, her eyes locked on Aarav's. "But it's like trying to solve a puzzle with missing pieces. I'm not even sure who I am anymore."

Kiyana's eyes refocused on Aarav's, her expression a mix of emotions. "After the accident... I don't remember much," she said, her voice soft. "But Riyan, my best friend, took me in. He brought me here to London and took care of me."

"...I'm going to marry Riyan after this event," Kiyana said, her voice carrying a note of finality.

Aarav's eyes flashed with a mix of emotions, his jaw clenched in frustration. "You're committing to a lifetime with him?" he asked, his voice tinged with a hint of disappointment.

Kiyana nodded, a small smile on her face. "Yes,

I am. He's been with me through everything... and I owe him my life."

Aarav's gaze pierced hers, his eyes searching for a glimmer of uncertainty. "Do you truly love him, Kiyana?" he asked, his voice low and husky.

She paused, a moment of uncertainty clouding her features. "Riyan... he's always been there. My best friend. He's always looked out for me, cared for me. And he... he feels strongly for me. And he loves me a lot."

Aarav's voice held a sharp edge. "People who are in love say 'we love each other,' not just 'he loves me."

Kiyana's expression shifted, as if a thought had just struck her.

Kiyana: "Well, I guess you have a better understanding about love... then explain it to me."

Aarav: "Yeah, I'd love to."

"Love is a mystery that has captivated our hearts for centuries. We've heard the saying 'love is blind,' *but I believe it's a choice to see beyond the imperfections, to cherish the flaws, and to accept someone wholeheartedly.* It's the ability to love someone at their lowest, when the world around them seems vulnerable.

It's the quiet moments, the stolen glances, the whispered promises that make love so extraordinary. Love is when you can sit in silence with that person, watching the sunset, feeling the warmth of their presence, and needing no words to express the depth of your emotions. It's when you can listen to them without getting bored, when their happiness becomes your own.

Love is a fastened heartbeat, the nervous excitement, and the calmness that follows. It's the feeling of being home, of being exactly where you're meant to be. It's the gentle breeze that soothes our soul, the thoughtful gestures that make us feel seen.

(Kiyana and Aarav spoke in unison)

*L*ove is a choice to let go, forgive, and to love unconditionally. It's a journey that requires courage, vulnerability, and an open heart."

Kiyana's eyes widened in shock as she stared at Aarav, her voice barely above a whisper. *"How did I...?"*

Aarav's face broke into a soft, gentle smile, his eyes crinkling at the corners. *"These are your words, love,"* he said, *his voice smooth and resonant. "How would you forget them?"*

Kiyana's eyes searched Aarav's, sensing a deep connection between them. *"I feel like I've known you my whole life,"* she said, her voice barely above a whisper.

Aarav's eyes locked onto hers, his gaze burning with an intensity that made her heart skip a beat. *"Maybe you have,"* he said, his voice deep and soothing

As the evening sky dawned, casting a soft pink glow over the forest, Aarav and Kiyana sat in silence, the sound of the waterfall creating a soothing melody in the background.

As they prepared to leave, Aarav reached out, offering Kiyana a gentle hand up. She accepted, her fingers intertwining with his as she rose to her feet.

Their palms touched, sending a spark of electricity through both of them. For a moment, they just stood there, hands clasped, eyes locked in a silent understanding.

As they walked back to the event's place, the silence between them was awkward, the air thick with unspoken emotions.

After dinner, they bid each other good night, their eyes locking in a brief, intense gaze.

"Good night, Kiyana," Aarav said, his voice gentle and intimate.

"Good night, Aarav," Kiyana replied, her voice barely above a whisper.

As they parted ways, the darkness seemed to swallow them whole, leaving only the echoes of their unspoken emotions.

Day: 4

While Kiyana and Aarav were enjoying the art event, Riyan was miles away, his brow furrowed in concentration. He sat in a dimly lit room, the glow of a computer screen illuminating his face. He was constantly on his phone, exchanging messages with someone named Marcus. "Any updates?" he typed, his fingers tapping impatiently.

Marcus's reply flashed on the screen: "Everything's going according to plan. Aria's details are coming together. It won't be long now."

Riyan's eyes narrowed. He was determined to keep Kiyana for himself, no matter the cost. He'd always been her protector, her best friend, and he couldn't imagine his life without her. He was involved in something dark, something he knew was wrong, but his obsession with Kiyana clouded his judgment. He was manipulating events, and studying Aria's past, all to ensure Kiyana stayed with him after the event. He told himself it was love, but deep down, he knew it was something else entirely.

The bonfire crackled, casting a warm glow on the faces gathered around. Aarav, with a knowing smile, handed Kiyana a steaming mug. "I made your favorite tea," he said.

Kiyana took a sip, her eyes widening. "Oh my goodness, Aarav! I'm going to get addicted to this."

Aarav winked. "Some addictions are good for you, I guess."

Kiyana laughed, shaking her head. "Oh, God, Aarav! I hate you for your cheesy lines."

He grinned, his voice soft. "Hate you too," he replied, the words laced with a warmth that didn't sound like hate at all.

Their conversation flowed easily, and Aarav asked, "So, what's your favorite music?"

Kiyana's eyes lit up. "Oh, I love 90s Bollywood classics. You know, Kishore Kumar, Jagjit Singh ji…"

"Lata Mangeshkar ji," Aarav added, his voice filled with genuine appreciation.

"Exactly!" Kiyana exclaimed, her voice filled with passion. "Their songs, even today, they just… they touch your soul."Aarav added, his voice filled with genuine appreciation. "Those songs… They're timeless."

"Exactly!" Kiyana agreed, her voice filled with passion. "They speak to something deep inside."

"That's interesting," Aarav said, a thoughtful look on his face. "Even I love them. In fact, I can play guitar. How about a little concert tonight?"

Kiyana's eyes sparkled with excitement. "Really? That would be amazing!"

Nancy, hearing their conversation, smiled brightly. "Guys, we have two beautiful Indian souls here who are going to bring our bonfire night to life with some great songs! Let's give them a warm welcome!"

Aarav picked up his guitar, and the first chords of "*Yeh Raatein, Yeh Mausam, Nadi Ka Kinaraa*" *(These nights, this weather, the riverbank).*filled the air. Kiyana joined in, her voice blending perfectly with his. "*Kaha do dilon ne ke milkar kabhi hum na honge juda.*"*(Two hearts said we'd never be apart).*

They moved seamlessly into "Bade Ache Lagte Hai." Aarav sang, "*Bade ache lagte hai... yeh dharti, yeh nadiyan, yeh raina.*"*(They feel very good... this earth, these rivers, this rain).*

Kiyana, her eyes twinkling, asked, "*Aur?*"*(And)*

Aarav, his gaze fixed on her, sang softly, "*Aur tum.*"*(And you) The crowd erupted in applause, their voices filled with joy.*

"Now, Kiyana, your turn!" someone called out.

Kiyana took a deep breath and began to sing "*Tera Mujhse Hai Pehle Ka Naata Koi.*"*(There's a connection between us from before).*Her voice was filled with emotion, captivating everyone. "*Yunhi nahi dil lubhata koi*" *(Not just anyone can charm the heart).*

Everyone was surprised, and Nancy praised them for the beautiful performance.

As the night deepened, the mood shifted to dancing. A slow, romantic song, "*Kabhi kabhi mere dil mein khayal aata hai.., ke jaise tujhko banaya gaya hai mere liye.*"

(Sometimes, a thought comes to my mind, that perhaps you were made for me.) began to play.

Aarav, his eyes searching hers, asked softly, "Miss Ma'am, would you care to dance?"

Kiyana nodded, her breath catching in her throat. Aarav gently took her hand and pulled her close. His hand rested lightly on her waist, and she felt a warmth spread through her. She leaned into him, feeling surprisingly comfortable in his arms. They swayed to the music, their eyes locked in a silent conversation. Kiyana felt a strange sense of familiarity, as if she were reliving a memory. *Their eyes held tears, doubts, and secrets threatening to spill out.* In his arms, she felt a sense of calm and peace she hadn't felt in a long time. It was perfect.

As they swayed to the music, Aarav's eyes sparkled with mischief. "Look at the sky," he whispered, his breath tickling Kiyana's ear. "The stars came out just to catch a glimpse of your smile."

Kiyana's cheeks flushed a deep crimson as she gazed up at the starry sky. She couldn't help but smile, and Aarav's eyes crinkled at the corners as he grinned.

"You're beautiful when you smile," he whispered, his voice smooth and velvety. Kiyana's heart skipped a beat as Aarav drew her closer, their bodies swaying in perfect harmony.

In that moment, everything else faded away, leaving only the two of them, lost in the music and the warmth of each other's presence.

From the breeze that carries her world

Dear moonlight,

Yesterday, by the waterfall, Aarav and I shared our stories, our pasts, our fears. It was like we were two old souls, connecting on a deeper level. And when we talked about love, I was amazed to find that our thoughts were in unison. "How's that possible?" I asked, and he just smiled.

But what really struck me was our shared taste in music. We both love 90's classics - the same bands, the same songs. It's like we're connected by an invisible thread.

I keep thinking about the choices we made tonight. The chai we shared, the music we danced to, the sky we gazed up at... it all felt like we were choosing each other, choosing this moment, choosing us.

He asked me to dance. I felt a flutter in my chest as I nodded, my heart racing with excitement. As we swayed to the music, I felt surprisingly comfortable in his arms. The height difference between us was adorable - he could whisper in my ear, his warm breath sending shivers down my spine. I loved the way he held me, the way our bodies moved in perfect harmony. It was like we were made to dance together. And when he whispered sweet nothings in my ear, I felt my heart melt.

I'm scared, I won't deny it. I'm scared of what this means and what might happen next. But at the same time, I'm excited. I feel alive, like I've been sleepwalking through life and have finally awakened.

I don't know what tomorrow will bring, but for the first time in a long time, I feel like I'm exactly where I'm meant to be.

Yours truly,
Kiyana

Day: 5

The fifth evening of the event arrived, and a gentle breeze carried the scent of the sea. As the sun dipped below the horizon, casting a warm, golden glow, Kiyana appeared. Aarav's breath caught in his throat. She was wearing a blue saree, a shade that seemed to mirror the twilight sky. Silver designs shimmered across the fabric, catching the light with every soft movement. Her hair, usually loose, was styled gracefully, and her eyes sparkled like the distant stars. She looked breathtaking, adorable, everything.

Aarav's heart skipped a beat as he approached her, his eyes drinking in the sight of her beauty. He wore his favorite white shirt, the one Kiyana had always loved. As they met, Aarav felt like he was drowning in the depths of her eyes.

"Kiyana," he breathed, his voice a little shaky.

he said, stepping closer, "you look like a dream. A beautiful, captivating dream."

He gently tucked a stray strand of hair behind her ear, his fingers brushing softly against her cheek.

"You're quite the charmer tonight," she teased, a blush coloring her cheeks.

"Only for you," he murmured.

The evening's program was a poetry session. "Ready to share your words?" Aarav asked, his heart beating a little faster.

"As ready as I'll ever be," Kiyana replied, a hint of nervousness in her voice.

As Aarav took the stage, his mind drifted back to this very day, the 17th of November, five years ago. It was the day he had confessed his feelings to her, a memory etched in his heart. His poem, a mix of longing and hope, carried the weight of those years.

As Aarav began to recite his poem, his voice was like a gentle breeze on a summer's day. Kiyana's eyes locked onto his, and she felt a sudden jolt of flashbacks. The words he spoke seemed to resonate deep within her, like a whispered secret only she could hear.

Aarav's eyes never left hers, his gaze burning with an intensity that made her heart skip a beat. His words wove a spell around her, transporting her to a place where time stood still.

When it all started

In the realm of our love, you may not even know the day
The moment when it all began in a magical way

The day when everything felt like sweet sixteen
A moment cherished in a gentle Blue scene
When my heartbeats felt really keen
Oh my lord, I just love this serene

The day when our eyes met for the very first time
The day my heart whispered this is love sublime
The day when my soul reached cloud nine
The day when you became my reason,my rhyme

Through the Rhythm and beats our friendship took flight,
As the 90's melodies filled our hearts with delight,
With Every lyric sung we found a connection,
A timeless bond, a musical affection.

From that day my pen danced for you
Verses of love pure and true
Countless times I tried to let go..
Yet your essence my heart's echo

Five years have flown by,
my heart is still not done with you
In the silent language of my eyes,
my love continues to renew

My heart would never dare to fall for someone who isn't you
With every falling star, I would always wish for you
In the realm of our love, you may not even know the day
The moment when it all began in a magical way

As Aarav finished his poem, Kiyana's eyes welled up with tears. She didn't know why, but something about his words had touched a deep chord within her. She felt seen, heard, and understood in a way she never had before.

The room erupted into applause, but Kiyana's eyes never left Aarav's. She felt a connection that went beyond words, a connection that spoke directly to her soul.

Now it was Kiyana's turn to recite her poem. She took a deep breath, her voice trembling slightly as she began to speak. But as she looked into Aarav's eyes, she felt a surge of confidence, a sense that she was exactly where she was meant to be.

Lost love

My heart skips a beat when I think of you,
Like I've known you my whole life, but we've just met, too.
It's as if the universe whispered your name in my ear,
And suddenly, I feel like I've been loving you for years.

Finding you feels like coming home,
to a place I've never been,
Like I've been searching for you my whole life,
 but didn't know where to begin.
Your smile, your laugh, your eyes... they all feel so familiar,
Like I've seen them in my dreams, or in a past life's memorial

My soul recognizes yours, like an old friend I've missed,
Like we've shared a thousand lifetimes, and our love has been forever fixed.
The universe brought us here, to this moment in time,
Where our hearts collide, and our love becomes forever aligned.

In your arms, I feel like I'm exactly where I'm meant to be,
Like our love is a missing piece I've been searching for, and now it's finally me.
I feel seen, heard, and understood, like you know my soul,
Like our love is a symphony, and our hearts are beating in perfect goal.

The room was transfixed as Kiyana's words poured out like a river, each one a celebration to the power of love and connection. When she finished, the room erupted into applause once more, but this time, it was Aarav's eyes that shone with tears.

At that moment, it was clear that something special had happened. Something that went beyond words, beyond poetry, and beyond the confines of the room. Something that would stay with them forever.

Kiyana's poem was a gentle exploration of emotions, a slow, unfolding realization of love. Aarav felt a flutter in his chest as she spoke, her words painting a picture of a heart gradually falling, unknowingly.

They sat together on the sea shore, the sound of the waves crashing against the rocks as they held their journals. Kiyana turned to Aarav, her eyes sparkling with curiosity.

"Your poem... was it about the love of your life?" she asked, her voice barely above a whisper.

Aarav's heart skipped a beat. "Yes, it was."

Kiyana's eyes searched his face. "Why didn't you move on? It's been five years."

Aarav's voice was low and husky. "I loved her, Kiyana. I still love her. True love isn't about how long you wait; it's about how strong you hold."

Kiyana's face softened, her eyes shining with emotion. "The girl you loved is the luckiest."

Aarav's smile was a gentle correction. "She still is. Or rather, I'm the lucky one *to have found her again.*"

Kiyana's voice was laced with a mix of hope and uncertainty as she turned to Aarav. "I guess with time, everything will be back to normal."

Aarav's eyes clouded over, his gaze drifting into the distance. "You know what they say," he began, his voice low and introspective. *"Time heals all our wounds… but they never admit the fact that time doesn't truly heal. It just hurts so much until we can no longer feel."*

The words hung in the air, a poignant reminder that some scars never fully fade. Kiyana's eyes locked onto Aarav's, and for a moment, they just looked at each other, the only sound the quiet beating of their hearts.

As they sat together in comfortable silence, the moon rising high in the sky, Aarav felt a sense of peace wash over him. They talked about their journals, their love for writing, and the solace they found in the written word.

Their conversation drifted to their journals.

"Why do you write?" Kiyana asked, her eyes reflecting the moonlight.

"It was her tradition," Aarav said softly, "and it brings me peace."

"And you?" he asked.

"It's the only place I can be completely myself," she replied, her voice barely above a whisper. "Where my confusing thoughts feel safe, listened to."

As the night wore on, they sat together in silence, the only sound the gentle lapping of the waves against the shore. The moon cast its silvery glow over the water, and Aarav felt like he was drowning in the depths of Kiyana's eyes.

Finally, Kiyana broke the silence. "Aarav, you're fluent in silence."

Aarav's smile was a flirtatious whisper. "Yeah, I am. Thanks for the compliment, Miss Ma'am. I'll stay happy for the next two weeks, at least."

Kiyana's laughter was a musical whisper. "Oh God, Aarav. Good night."

"Good night Kiya",aarav replied.

As they parted ways, Aarav felt like he was walking on air, his heart soaring with a sense of hope. *The moon and stars twinkled above, while thinking about what they just witnessed was incredibly beautiful*

Day: 6

The sun shone brightly in the sky, casting a warm glow over the landscape. A gentle breeze rustled the leaves of the trees, carrying the sweet scent of blooming flowers. It was a perfect day, with just a few puffy white clouds drifting lazily across the blue expanse.

As the lunch hour drew to a close, the group began to stir, their faces relaxed and content after a satisfying meal. The atmosphere was tranquil, with the sound of laughter and conversation carrying on the breeze. Aarav and Kiyana strolled out of the dining area, their eyes meeting for a brief moment before Kiyana looked away, a hint of a smile playing on her lips. Little did she know, Aarav had a surprise waiting for her, one that would bring a sparkle to her eyes and a smile to her face.

Aarav, with a nervous flutter in his stomach, slipped away to meet Nancy near the quiet corner of the event area.

Nancy: Hey Aarav, what's up?

Aarav: Not much, Nancy. Just needed to talk to you about something.

Nancy: What is it?

Aarav: I want to surprise Kiyana with a special food event. She loves Pani Puri, and I thought it would be awesome to set up a make-and-eat station.

Nancy beamed, "Aarav, that's so sweet! You're really head over heels for her, aren't you?" She gave him a playful nudge.

Nancy: That's so sweet! I'd be happy to help you arrange it.

Aarav blushed, a warm, rosy hue spreading across his cheeks. "Maybe a little," he mumbled, his gaze drifting towards where Kiyana was standing a little distance away.

Meanwhile, Kiyana, from a short distance, saw them talking. She saw Nancy's smile, and a weird little feeling popped up inside her. It was like a tiny, green monster of… well, maybe a little jealousy.

As Nancy walked away, Kiyana approached Aarav, her steps a little too quick, her voice a little too sharp. "What were you two talking about?" she asked, her eyes narrowing slightly.

Aarav, caught off guard, stammered, "Oh, nothing much. She was just, uh, admiring my… looks." He tried to play it cool, but a nervous laugh betrayed him.

Kiyana rolled her eyes. "Yeah, yeah, I'm sure." She crossed her arms, a hint of annoyance in her voice.

Aarav, sensing her unease, teased, "Are you jealous, Kiya?"

"Jealous? Me? Don't be silly," she retorted, turning away abruptly. "Why would I be jealous?"

"Oh god, this girl never admits when she's jealous... something that has never changed, and I guess will never change!"

He followed her, his steps light.

"By the way," he said, catching up to her, "Kiya…"

"Kiyana," she corrected him, her voice a little sharper than she intended.

"Right, Kiyana," he said, his voice soft. "I thought, now that we're friends, I could call you Kiya." He paused, his eyes twinkling. "You look really cute when you're jealous."

Kiyana ignored him, a small pout forming on her lips. "Whatever," she muttered, a hint of a smile tugging at the corner of her mouth.

"Oh, it's just Kiya and her whatever against me," Aarav thought to himself with a hint of amusement.

Aarav, undeterred, gently grabbed her arm. "I have a surprise for you," he said, his voice filled with excitement.

"I hate surprises," she grumbled, but her eyes betrayed her curiosity.

"And I love when you hate something," he teased, his laughter light and carefree.

Kiyana rolled her eyes, but a small smile played on her lips. "What is it?"

"You'll love it, trust me," Aarav said, his eyes crinkling at the corners.

Just then, Nancy's voice rang out, announcing the day's activity. "Today, we're going to have a make-and-eat food competition! You can create your own dishes and have fun while doing it."

Aarav, with a flourish, gestured towards a table laden with plates and ingredients. "Miss Ma'am, your surprise!"

Kiyana's eyes widened. On the table were all the ingredients for Pani Puri: crispy puris, tangy tamarind water, spicy filling, and sweet chutney. Her face lit up like a child .

"Oh my god, Aarav! You know what I love, love, LOVE – Pani puri!"

She gave him a quick, impulsive hug, then eagerly began preparing her own.

"You don't have to make it," Aarav said gently, his eyes fixed on her. "Just sit and enjoy the view. I'll make it for you ma'am."

With graceful movements, he assembled the Pani Puri, filling each puri with the perfect balance of flavors. The crispy shells, the tangy water, the sweet and spicy fillings, all combined to create a burst of deliciousness.

Finally, he handed her a steaming plate, the aroma of spices and chutneys wafting up to tease her senses. Kiyana ate each Pani Puri with delight, her face glowing with happiness. Her eyes closed in rapture as the flavors exploded on her tongue."This is the best!" she exclaimed, her eyes sparkling.

She was the happiest girl in the world, her heart full of gratitude for this small, thoughtful gesture. "Thank you, Aarav," she said, her voice barely above a whisper.

Aarav's smile softened, his eyes drinking in the sight of her radiant face. "Anytime, Kiya,"

Aarav watched her, his heart swelling with affection. "Kiya," he thought, *"I could fall in love with you every day, every moment."* He adored her carefree joy, the way her eyes lit up with simple pleasures.

They spent the rest of the afternoon laughing and making Pani Puri, their playful banter filling the air. The sun dipped below the horizon, painting the sky in hues of orange and pink, as they shared the delicious treat. Aarav's surprise had been a resounding success, leaving Kiyana with a warm, fuzzy feeling and a lingering taste of tangy, spicy goodness.

From the breeze that carries her world

Dear moonlight,

These past two days have been a whirlwind of emotions. It started with Aarav reciting that beautiful poem. I couldn't help but feel a connection to the words, and to him. We had a deep conversation by the sea shore, watching the sunset together. Time flew by, and before I knew it, the evening had turned into night.

And then, today, Aarav surprised me with Pani puri. It was such a thoughtful gesture, and I couldn't help but feel a little jealous. I don't know why, but it bothered me to see him talking to Nancy earlier. I tried to brush it off, but the feeling lingered.

I also had a chance to talk to Riyan today. He's been checking in on me, making sure I'm doing okay. We had a nice conversation on the phone, and it made me realize that I'll be seeing him soon. The thought of our marriage after this event is looming over me. I'm caught between the familiarity of my future with Riyan and the excitement of these new moments with Aarav.

As I navigate these conflicting emotions, I'm trying to stay present and not get lost in the uncertainty of what's to come.

Yours truly,
Kiyana

From the wind that Whispers his name

Dear starlight,

These six days have been a journey of discovery, of connection, of emotions. Every day, I feel like I'm a little closer to her. Kiyana. The mere thought of her name makes my heart skip a beat.

But it's not just about Kiyana. I've also been constantly checking in on Aria, my little sister. She's under Arjun's protection, and I know she's safe. Still, I worry. I've been in touch with her, and she reassures me that she's fine, that her health is perfectly fine now. Hearing that makes me happy. I just want what's best for her.

And then, there's Riyan. I'm aware of him, of the fact that he's a part of Kiyana's life. But I'm not intimidated. I've got a plan, a way to deal with him. I'm not worried... yet.

And talking about her, seeing her happy makes me happy. I'm lost in her beauty, in her happiness, in everything about her. I feel like I'm drowning in the depths of her eyes, and I don't want to be saved.

My goal is simple: to help her remember, to bring back the memories we shared, bit by bit. And if that means being patient, being gentle, and being kind, then so be it. I'm willing to take that chance, for her, for us, and for the memories we once shared.

Yours truly,
Aarav

Riyan - Aria…

Riyan, his jaw clenched, spoke into his phone. "Marcus, give me Aria's exact location. Now."

"She's at a temporary flat, heading towards Dr. Arjun's clinic for a check-up," Marcus's voice echoed through the speaker.

Riyan's eyes narrowed. "Perfect." He started his car, the engine roaring to life. "I'll handle this myself."

Aria, behind the wheel of her sleek car, felt a sense of unease. She was a force to be reckoned with, strong-willed, and possessed the same unwavering determination as her brother. Her blue eyes, usually calm, held an intensity that could make anyone pause.

As she navigated the city streets, she noticed a car speeding towards her, its headlights piercing the afternoon haze. Instinctively, she gripped the steering wheel, her senses on high alert. Just as the car was about to collide, she executed a perfect drift, her car swerving gracefully. The other car, equally agile, mirrored her move.

For a fleeting second, their eyes met. Aria's intense gaze locked with Riyan's, a spark of recognition flashing in her eyes. She knew that face.

The air filled with the acrid smell of burning rubber and exhaust fumes. Before Aria could react, the car sped away, disappearing into the maze of city streets.

"Who was that?" she muttered, her heart pounding. *"Riyan!"*

Aria, her adrenaline surging, slammed her foot on the accelerator, chasing after the disappearing car. "I'm not letting him get away this time."

Riyan, glancing in his rearview mirror, felt a surge of both admiration and apprehension. "This girl is something else," he thought. "Her driving skills are insane." He wasn't afraid of confronting Aria, but he was terrified of what Kiyana might think if she found out. "If she knows who I am, she might put everything in danger."

He took a sharp turn, weaving through the traffic, trying to lose her. Aria, however, was relentless, her blue eyes fixed on his car, her determination unwavering.

After a long chase, Riyan finally managed to lead her to the opposite side of the city, a less crowded area. He stopped his car, and Aria pulled up behind him, her engine idling.

"Riyan," she said, her voice sharp, "What do you think you're doing?"

Riyan stepped out of his car, his expression calm. "Aria, we need to talk."

"Talk? You tried to run me off the road!" she exclaimed, her eyes blazing.

"I didn't," he said, his voice low. "It was an accident."

Aria narrowed her eyes. "An accident? Don't lie to me."

"Okay fine, it wasn't an accident. But it was a warning," Riyan said, stepping closer. "Stay away from Kiyana and tell your brother to stay away from her."

Aria's eyes widened." No, he won't."

Riyan's face hardened. "Just stay away. For your own good."

"Or what?" Aria challenged, her voice filled with defiance.

Riyan looked at her, his expression unreadable. "You don't want to find out."

Day: 7

The seventh day of the event unfolded with a gentle hum, a stark contrast to the undercurrents swirling beneath the surface.

Nancy's cheerful voice rang out, "Today, we're crafting gifts for our team partners! It's pottery day, everyone!" The tables were laden with clay, water, and tools, ready for the participants to mold their artistic visions.

Kiyana and Aarav settled at their station, a comfortable silence settling between them. But Kiyana, with her keen intuition, noticed a subtle tension in Aarav's demeanor. "Everything alright?" she asked, her eyes searching for him.

Aarav's eyes clouded over for a moment before he smiled. "Yeah, it's just that my sister, Aria, she's here for her treatment. She's fine, but she didn't pick up my call, and I'm a little worried."

Kiyana's expression softened. "Oh, I hope she feels better soon. Don't worry, she'll be okay."

Aarav's eyes locked onto hers, and he felt a surge of gratitude. *How did this girl have the power to sense my emotions so accurately ! She had this incredible gift for knowing exactly what I needed to hear, exactly when I needed to hear it."*

He smiled, feeling a sense of relief wash over him. "Thanks, Kiyana. Let's focus on making something beautiful."

"After you, Miss Ma'am," he said, gesturing to the clay with a playful bow.

Kiyana's hands moved deftly, shaping the clay into what promised to be a beautiful creation. But as she worked, her brow furrowed in concentration, her lips pursed in frustration. The clay refused to cooperate, crumbling beneath her fingers.

Aarav watched, a hint of amusement dancing in his eyes. "You need my help, Kiya?" he asked, his voice low and gentle.

Kiyana's eyes flashed with determination. "No, thanks, Aarav. I'll try again." Her hands moved swiftly, reshaping the clay, but again, it failed to hold its form.

Aarav waited patiently, knowing Kiyana's perfectionist streak. He'd seen her get frustrated before, her patience wearing thin when things didn't go her way.

The third attempt ended in disaster, the clay splattering everywhere. Kiyana's eyes sparkled with annoyance, her cheeks flushing with frustration.

Aarav couldn't help but chuckle. "What are your current thoughts about me helping you, Miss Ma'am?" he teased, his eyes crinkling at the corners.

Kiyana's smile was a mixture of anger and amusement. "Yeah, help me with this, Aarav."

Aarav's eyes gleamed with triumph. *Oh, I knew this was coming*, he thought to himself. "Let me help you with it, Kiya," he said, his voice low and smooth, as he stepped closer, his hands reaching out to guide hers.

As Aarav's hands wrapped around Kiyana's, guiding her fingers through the clay, she felt a spark of electricity run through her body. His chest pressed gently against her back, his warm breath whispering against her ear. The mud squished between their hands, a tactile reminder of their closeness.

Together, they shaped the clay, their hands moving in sync. The silence between them was palpable, but it wasn't uncomfortable. Instead, it felt intimate, like they were sharing a secret.

Kiyana's heart beat faster, her senses heightened. She felt Aarav's warmth, his strength, and his gentle guidance. It was as if time had slowed down, and all that mattered was this moment, this touch, and this connection.

Kiyana, her focus wavering, couldn't help but admire Aarav's concentration. The way his brow furrowed, the gentle movements of his hands, it all seemed to draw her in.

 Aarav couldn't help but tease her, his voice low and playful.

"One more minute…" he whispered, his eyes locked on hers.

Kiyana's gaze met his, a hint of curiosity in her eyes. "What?" she asked, her voice barely above a whisper.

Aarav's grin was mischievous. "One more minute you keep looking at me like this, and boom..you'll fall in love with me."

Kiyana's laughter was instant, her cheeks flushing with amusement. "Shut up, Aarav!" she playfully scolded, her eyes still shining with mirth.

Aarav chuckled, his eyes crinkling at the corners. "Just saying," he teased, his voice dripping with amusement.

They chatted and laughed, their hands working together, until a beautiful pot emerged from the clay.

"I'll paint it for you," Kiyana offered, her eyes shining.

"That would be perfect," Aarav replied, his gaze lingering on her.

The air crackled with unspoken emotions. They sat close, their hands still slightly damp, their eyes locked in a silent conversation. Aarav gently tucked a stray strand of hair behind Kiyana's ear, the simple gesture sending shivers down her spine.

Nancy's throat-clearing broke the spell, shattering the intimate moment between Kiyana and Aarav. "Lovely!" Nancy exclaimed, her eyes fixed on the pot, a warm smile spreading across her face. "It truly reflects your combined efforts."

Kiyana's cheeks flushed with a soft blush, her eyes darting to Aarav's, then quickly away. Aarav, sensing her discomfort, offered a gentle hand, helping her to her feet. His touch was brief, but the spark of electricity lingered.

As the group gathered around, admiring their handiwork, the atmosphere transformed into a warm, convivial gathering. Laughter and shared stories filled the air, the scent of wet clay and creativity lingering in the background.

Yet, beneath the surface, a subtle undercurrent of tension hummed, a silent promise of the drama to come. The unspoken emotions, the unresolved conflicts, and the unrequited feelings all simmered, waiting to erupt into a passionate storm. For now, the group remained oblivious, lost in the joy of the moment, but the seeds of turmoil had been sown.

Riyan - Aria …

Aria, her blue eyes blazing, stood her ground. "Do whatever you want, Riyan. I'm not afraid of your tricks."

But as she spoke, a wave of dizziness washed over her. The world around her seemed to blur, and she swayed, her strength suddenly failing her. She felt herself falling, a sense of panic rising within her.

Riyan, his expression shifting from stern to alarmed, reacted instantly. He caught her just before she hit the ground, his arms wrapping around her. "Aria!" he exclaimed, his voice filled with concern.

He lifted her gently, his touch surprisingly tender. Her skin was cool, and her breathing was shallow. He noticed a faint bruise on her temple, a sign of a recent fall.

A wave of worry washed over him. He couldn't leave her like this. Ignoring the tension between them, he carried her to his car and drove quickly to his office, a sleek, modern space in a quiet part of the city.

He laid her gently on a plush sofa in his office, his eyes fixed on her pale face. "Aria," he said softly, shaking her gently. "Can you hear me?"

Aria's eyelids fluttered open, her gaze unfocused. "Riyan?" she whispered, her voice weak.

"You fainted," he said, his voice low. "You're not well."

Aria tried to sit up, but a wave of dizziness forced her back down. "I'm fine," she insisted, her voice barely a whisper.

 He paused, his eyes narrowing. "You'll follow what I say, or else…"

Aria's eyes flashed with defiance, even in her weakened state. "Or else what, Riyan? You think you can control me?"

she retorted, her voice regaining its strength. "I told you, I'm not afraid of your tricks."

She tried to rise again, but Riyan gently pushed her back down. "Just rest," he said, his voice softer this time. "You need to take care of yourself."

"Why do you care?" Aria asked, her voice laced with suspicion. "You tried to run me off the road."

Riyan's expression remained unreadable. "That was a warning," he said, his voice low and mysterious. "But I didn't want to hurt you."

"A warning about what?" Aria demanded, her eyes searching for him. "What are you hiding, Riyan?"

Riyan looked at her, his expression a mix of concern and something else, something she couldn't quite decipher. "Some things are better left unknown," he said, his voice laced with a hint of danger. "Just trust me, Aria. You'll be safer if you do what I say."

"You're a devil, Riyan," Aria said, her voice trembling slightly, but her eyes still held a spark of defiance.

Riyan's lips curled into a chilling smirk. "I always thought my life was like a story of heroes and villains. But now I understand, it's a double-sided coin, and I always choose the villainy."

A shiver ran down Aria's spine. "You can't control what's not in your hands," she said, her voice low.

Riyan's eyes darkened. "I love Kiyana," he said, his voice laced with a chilling intensity. "And I'll do anything to keep her with me." A glint of something truly unsettling flickered in his eyes.

Aria stared at him, her heart pounding. "That's not love, Riyan," she said, her voice filled with a quiet horror. "That's an obsession."

He looked at her, and his smile faded. "You don't understand," he said, his voice low and dangerous. "You don't understand what I'm capable of."

Day: 8

The morning air was crisp, with a chilling breeze that carried the whispers of the mountains. Kiyana stood at the edge of the campsite, sipping the warm chai Aarav had made for her. He was busy journaling at the table, his pen moving swiftly across the pages.

As she gazed out at the breathtaking view, a sudden gust of wind swept through, rustling the pages of Aarav's journal. A picture slipped out, dancing in the air before landing at Kiyana's feet.

She picked it up, her eyes widening as she took in the familiar drawing. A flashback hit her like a ton of bricks. She remembered owning a necklace with the same design, the one her mother had taken away five years ago, saying it would bother her.

The memories came flooding back – the feel of the necklace against her skin, the way it sparkled in the light. Kiyana's eyes snapped back to Aarav, who was still busy in the kitchen. "You draw sketches?" she asked, trying to sound casual.

Aarav's response was immediate. "No, I don't. But my love used to." He turned around, his eyes locking onto hers. "Why do you ask?"

Kiyana's heart skipped a beat. She quickly shoved the picture into her pocket, trying to play it cool. "No, just asking... randomly, you know."

Later, back in her tent, the image of the necklace wouldn't leave her mind. As she closed her eyes, a vivid flashback surged through her. This time, there were colors – warm, vibrant hues. *A boy, his face obscured, gently placed the necklace around her neck. His hands, tender and loving, caressed her hair, and then, a soft kiss on her neck.*

The flashback vanished, leaving her breathless and confused. She replayed the past few days in her mind, the moments with Aarav, the laughter, the shared glances, the growing connection. It hit her like a wave – she was falling in love with him.

But there was a knot of fear in her stomach. Riyan. His face flashed in her mind, his eyes dark and intense, the promise of marriage hanging heavy in the air. She remembered the strange determination in his voice, the way he looked at her.

Why do I feel so drawn to Aarav? she wondered, her mind a mess of conflicting emotions. And why does Riyan seem so… possessive?

She reached for her journal, her fingers trembling as she wrote:

From the breeze that carries her world

Dear moonlight,

Fate is a strange and twisted thing. Today, I saw a sketch, a necklace I recognized from a lifetime ago, or so it seems. It triggered something within me, a memory, a feeling I couldn't quite grasp. And then, the flashbacks, clearer this time, filled with warmth and love.

I've been trying to deny it, to push it away, but I can't anymore. I'm falling for Aarav. Hard. The way he looks at me, the way he makes me laugh, the way he cares, it's all so... familiar.

I don't understand what's happening. It's like my heart remembers something my mind has forgotten. The necklace, the flashbacks, the way I feel around Aarav... it's all so confusing. And then there's Riyan, his eyes, the promise, the way he looks at me. I feel trapped, like I'm caught between two worlds, two lives.

I'm falling for Aarav, and it terrifies me. I don't know why I feel such a pull to him, but it's like my soul recognizes him. But, Riyan is always there, in the back of my mind. He's like a storm cloud, always threatening.

I'm so confused. Is it possible? Could he be... the boy from my memories? The boy with the necklace? I don't know, but something deep within me tells me there's more to this than just a coincidence. I have to find out. I have to know the truth.

Yours truly,
Kiyana

Day: 9

T he morning air, usually crisp and refreshing, felt heavy, thick with unspoken dread. Riyan's voice, a cold, sharp blade, sliced through the silence of Aarav's phone. "Your dear sister, Aria, is currently… experiencing my hospitality."

Aarav's blood ran cold, his hands clenching into fists. "What did you do to her?" he growled, his voice a low, dangerous rumble. "Don't you dare lay a finger on her, Riyan, or I swear, I'll kill you."

Riyan's laughter, a dark, unsettling sound, echoed in Aarav's ear. "Oh, Aarav, you're positively glowing with rage. I must say, it suits you. The way you beg for her safety, it's… delightful. You want her back? A little visit to my office, perhaps? I'll be waiting."

Aarav's mind reeled with the consequences. He was too afraid to let anything happen to Aria. He was determined to save her life at any cost. "I'll be there," he snarled, his eyes welling up with tears.

Aarav quickly scribbled a note, his hand shaking with urgency. "Kiyana, I have an emergency. I'm leaving. Please take care. Sorry for leaving the event before we could meet again. - Aarav." He left his phone number at the bottom, hoping she would understand.

Meanwhile, Kiyana, her heart fluttering with anticipation, was ready to confess her feelings. She was eager to see Aarav. *Fate's cruel irony: Kiyana's memories of their all-consuming love had faded with time, yet her heart, once again, beat solely for him. Five years had passed, but the flame that once burned bright had merely smoldered, waiting to reignite. And now, as she fell deeply in love with the same person, she was oblivious to the fact that her heart had come full circle, back to the one who had once owned it entirely.*

But when she woke, his tent was empty, and the note was gone.

Unseen by Kiyana, Marcus, Riyan's trusted detective, had quietly intercepted the note, his fingers ripping it to pieces before casting it away, erasing the only trace of Aarav's message.

She asked Nancy about Aarav, but Nancy had no answers. Kiyana's excitement turned to confusion and then to a sharp pang of disappointment.

Then, her mother called, her voice heavy with a sorrow Kiyana couldn't comprehend. "Kiyana, my darling," her mother began, her voice trembling, "there are things you don't remember… things I should have told you sooner."

Kiyana's heart pounded. "What things, Mom?" she whispered, a knot of fear tightening in her chest.

Her mother hesitated, then spoke in a broken voice. "There's a reason you lost those memories, Kiyana. A reason you feel so drawn to Aarav, and a reason Riyan is so... protective."

Kiyana's breath caught in her throat. "What are you saying?" she asked, her voice barely audible.

"It's… complicated," her mother said, her voice strained. "Aarav… he was there. In your past. And Riyan… he was too."

Kiyana's mind reeled, a dizzying swirl of confusion and fear. "What does that mean?" she cried, her voice cracking.

Kiyana's parents had unknowingly become pawns in Riyan's game of deception. He had convinced them that Aarav was the culprit behind Kiyana's shattered past. Her mother, blinded by Riyan's influence, had willingly become a messenger of heartbreak.

With a heavy heart, she had told Kiyana the lie: "Aarav is the reason you lost your memories,kiya. He's the one who destroyed your life."

The words, laced with false truth, had pierced Kiyana's soul like a dagger.

Kiyana's phone slipped from her grasp, crashing to the ground. She sank down, tears streaming down her face.

"No," she whispered, her voice broken. "It can't be."

The moments with Aarav, the laughter, the shared secrets, the chai, the dances, everything flashed before her eyes. The boy she was about to confess her love to was the one who had taken her past.

"Why?" she cried, her voice raw with pain. "Why would he do this?"

Just as she thought she couldn't cry anymore, Riyan appeared beside her, his eyes blazing with an intensity that made her heart skip a beat.

Riyan's voice was low and husky, his words dripping with a possessiveness that sent shivers down her spine. "As long as I breathe, Kiyana, your tears are mine to wipe away. No one will ever hurt you again."

His eyes locked onto hers, burning with a fierce passion that seemed to sear her very soul. "*You're mine, Kiyana. Mine to protect, mine to love... and mine to avenge.*"

Riyan's whisper was a gentle breeze against Kiyana's ear, "In the shadows, secrets are kept... but I'll be your light, your truth." As he pulled her closer, his eyes gleamed with a subtle intensity, masking the darkness within - a devil's smile, hidden behind a savior's guise.

To himself, Riyan thought: "*Aarav, your hell is just beginning... and I'm the one who'll ignite the flames.*"

Kiyana: Betrayal of the heart

Kiyana sat by the window, the mountain view now a blur of colors, mirroring the chaos within her. Her heart was a battleground, torn between the love she couldn't forget and the reality she couldn't escape. Two days had passed since she'd last seen Aarav, and the silence was deafening. She'd waited, hoping against hope that he'd come back for her, that he'd fight for their love. That he would somehow make sense of the tangled mess her life had become. But the silence stretched, heavy and suffocating, crushing her spirit with each passing hour. The hours ticked by, and the only sound was the echo of her own heartbeat.

The laughter, the shared moments, the warmth of his smile—they all felt like distant echoes, fading into a painful memory. She'd confessed her feelings to the empty air, her heart a shattered mosaic of love and betrayal.

She picked up her phone, her fingers trembling as she dialed Riyan's number. "Riyan," she said, her voice hollow, "tomorrow. I'll marry you."

A chilling smile spread across Riyan's face. "Excellent," he said, his voice laced with a dark satisfaction. "I'll make all the arrangements. *Tomorrow, you'll be mine.*"

He'd made sure Aarav was occupied, his attention diverted by Aria's fragile health. He'd kept Aarav away, ensuring this moment, this twisted victory, was his. Aria, her health a delicate balance, was finally stable enough for Riyan to leave her to her own devices. He had come to the event to secure his prize.

Kiyana's eyes stung with unshed tears as she ended the call. She felt like she was drowning in a sea of despair, with no lifeline in sight. She'd built walls around her heart, hoping to keep the pain at bay. She was tired of the confusion, the uncertainty. She was tired of the waiting. She was tired of the pain.

She was tired of hoping. She wanted it all to end, and Riyan's offer was the only ending she could see. She would marry Riyan, and she would find some sort of peace in the ruins of her shattered heart. She looked out the window.

Tomorrow, she would marry Riyan, a man who didn't love her, but desired her with an intensity that scared her. Kiyana's heart wept for the love she'd lost, and the future she'd never have with Aarav.

Tomorrow, she would wear his ring, but she vowed, in the deepest part of her soul, that he would never own her heart.

From the breeze that carries her world

Dear moonlight,

We weren't a tale of forever, but a fleeting spark,
A forbidden love, hidden in the shadows of the dark.
Our story was a whispered secret, never meant to be told,
A chapter of bliss, before the final page grew old.

We were the moment before the storm, the calm before the pain,
A love that flourished in the darkness, but couldn't withstand the rain.
Our hearts beat as one, in the silence of the night,
But our love was a fragile flame that flickered out of sight.

We were a love letter, penned in the margins of life,
A secret kept, a promise broken, a goodbye without a strife.
Our love was a moment, a memory, a bittersweet refrain,
A story that was always meant to end, in sorrow and in pain.

There's no happily ever after, no fairy tale for us two,
Just a memory of what could've been, a love that shone true.
We were a brief, shining moment, a flash of pure delight,
A love that burned brightly, but burned out in the night.

I am left with fragments of us , shards of love so true
A puzzle I am trying to piece together but it is missing you ..
I am searching for a goodbye a closure to our tale
But like sand between my fingers it slips away leaving only frail

In this silence I hear your voice , a whispered goodbye,

A chance to make amends , to heal the tears I've cried,
But like the dream that fades at dawn , it vanishes into thin air leaving
me with just these fragments of us to hold and to share ..

Yours truly,
Kiyana

The threads of destiny…

Aarav's eyes scanned the crowded hallway, his heart racing with every passing second. He had to find Aria. Suddenly, he heard a faint cry for help. With a surge of adrenaline, Aarav rushed towards the sound and found Aria lying on the ground, her body trembling with fear.

"Aria!" Aarav exclaimed, scooping her up in his arms. "What happened?"

As he held her close, Aria's tears soaked into his shirt. "Riyan… I chased his car, Bhaiya," she stammered. "I wanted to talk to him, to understand why he's doing all this. We drove to the other side of the city, and then he stopped the car."

Aarav's grip on her tightened, his mind reeling with anger and worry. "What happened next?"

Aria's voice was barely above a whisper. "Riyan got out of the car, and we talked for a bit. But then… I don't know, Bhaiya. I just felt dizzy and fainted."

Aarav's expression turned skeptical. "And then Riyan took you to his office?"

Aria nodded, her eyes welling up with tears. "Yes, Bhaiya. He told me it was just a warning, that he didn't want to ruin my health."

Aarav's jaw clenched in anger. "He's a master manipulator, Aria. Don't trust him."

Aria's eyes locked onto Aarav's, a hint of determination in her voice. "I know, Bhaiya. But I think Riyan has a good side. I saw it today."

Aarav's curiosity was piqued. "What do you mean?"

Aria's voice was laced with a mix of emotions. "I think he's not all bad, Bhaiya. And I have a plan to use that to our advantage."

As Aarav listened to Aria's words, he couldn't help but feel a glimmer of hope.

Later that day, Aarav received a call from Riyan. His voice was cold and detached.

"Riyan," Aarav answered.

Riyan: "Aarav, Kiyana has willingly agreed to marry me tomorrow."

Riyan: "I'm securing my future. A future you can't touch."

Riyan's laughter sent a chill down Aarav's spine. "I'll write the future, Aarav."

"No," Aarav replied, his voice hardening. "It's already written. By fate. Trust me, Riyan. Soon, you'll realize how much of a devil you've become, consumed by your obsession."

Riyan: "Fate? Fate is what I make it."

Aarav: "No, Riyan. You're carving your own destruction. You'll see that soon enough."

Riyan: "Empty threats, Aarav. Enjoy your

delusions." (line goes dead)

As Aria watched Aarav's interaction with Riyan, she couldn't help but feel a sense of determination. She had a plan, and she was willing to risk everything to make it work.

"I'll change the course of this story, Bhaiya," Aria whispered *to herself. "I'll make sure that good wins over evil. And I'll start by using Riyan's good side to our advantage."*

With a newfound sense of purpose, Aria smiled to herself, ready to face whatever challenges lay ahead

The truth revealed…

The sun had set, casting a warm orange glow over the wedding venue. The air was alive with the sweet scent of flowers and the soft hum of chatter. But amidst the beauty and joy, a sense of heaviness settled over the decorations, as if the very atmosphere was weighed down by the significance of the day.

In her room, Kiyana stood before the mirror, her golden and red saree shimmering in the soft light. Her eyes, like two shimmering pools of water, seemed to hold a world of emotions within them. Tears, fears, and secrets all swirled together, threatening to spill over at any moment.

As she adjusted the delicate fabric, her gaze searched for someone who wasn't there. Her heart ached with a deep longing, and her eyes welled up with unshed tears.

"It was a day of eternal promises, yet I felt the weight of forever. The decorations shone bright, but my heart felt dull. I vowed to love, but feared I'd fail. The world was ready to celebrate our union, but I wondered if we were ready." Kiyana thought to herself.

Just then, a soft knock at the door broke the silence. "Kiyana?" Aria's voice called out.

Kiyana's eyes snapped towards the door, a hint of surprise on her face.

Aria slipped inside, her eyes widening as she took in Kiyana's stunning appearance. "Hii, kiya," she said, her voice barely above a whisper.

Kiyana's gaze met Aria's, and for a moment, time seemed to stand still. A strange, far-off look crept into Kiyana's eyes, as if memories long forgotten were rising to the surface.

And then, like a dam breaking, the floodgates of her mind opened. Memories of her wedding day, of Aarav by her side, of the accident, all came rushing back. Tears streamed down her face as she trembled, her voice barely audible.

"Aa... Aria..." she whispered.

Aria's eyes shone with tears as she wrapped Kiyana in a tight hug. "Finally, you got your memories back," she whispered.

As Kiyana's sobs subsided, Aria gently explained the truth. "Kiyana, bhaiya loves you so much. He's been searching for you everywhere. And you... you loved him too."

Kiyana's eyes, now red-rimmed from crying, locked onto Aria's, a glimmer of understanding sparking within them.

"I remember," she whispered, her voice barely audible. "I remember everything."

Aria's words spilled out in a rush, as if she'd been holding onto this secret for far too long. "Riyan, he was Bhaiya's rival, and their rivalry led him to plan an accident. The accident was meant for him, but you came in between, and… and the car hit you instead."

Kiyana's eyes widened in horror as the truth sank in.

Aria's voice cracked with emotion. "He is not a photographer, Kiya. He's a brain surgeon! He saved your life, but your parents were made to believe that bhaiya had ruined your life. It was all a lie. After that day, he couldn't bring himself to practice surgery again. The pain of losing you was too much. So, he took up photography instead, capturing moments that kept him close to you."

Kiyana's mind reeled as she processed the information. Riyan, the man she was about to marry, had ruined her life. He'd manipulated her parents, messed with her medications, and kept her away from Aarav.

Aria handed Kiyana a journal, its pages filled with Aarav's handwriting. "This is Bhaiya's journal. He wrote about his love for you, about how he never gave up hope of finding you again."

As Kiyana flipped through the pages, she saw photos of herself and Aarav, happy moments captured in time. Tears streamed down her face as she realized the truth. Her eyes widened in wonder. Every memory, every moment they'd shared, was meticulously documented. The notes, the poems she'd written for him, the drawing of the necklace he'd gifted her on her birthday… everything was there.

Aria's voice was barely above a whisper.

"Bhaiya's love for you never faded, Kiyana. He always woke up thinking that one day he'd find you again. And when he did, Riyan tried to repeat his wrongful intentions again."

Kiyana's eyes overflowed with tears as she realized the depth of Aarav's love for her. She'd never known, never suspected, that he'd held onto their memories so tightly.

Aria wrapped her arms around Kiyana, holding her close as she sobbed. "Let it all out, kiya. You've been carrying this burden for so long."

Kiyana's tears soaked into Aria's shoulder as she clung to her. "I'm so sorry, Aria. I'm so sorry I didn't remember. I'm sorry I was going to marry Riyan."

Aria's voice was soft and soothing. "Don't blame yourself, Kiyana. Don't blame your parents either. They were manipulated by Riyan, just like you were. This is all on him."

Kiyana pulled back, her eyes red-rimmed but determined. "I want to talk to him. I want to know why he did this."

Aria's expression turned grim. "Be careful, Kiyana. Riyan is ruthless."

In that moment I realised I had been living in a dream, a fantasy crafted by riyan's twisted hands.His name was a curse, a reminder of the hell he'd dragged us through.

Kiyana's eyes narrowed, her voice firm. "No more secrets, no more lies. I want to hear the truth from Riyan himself. Call him."

The ache of letting go: the freedom to fly …

Riyan entered the room, his eyes immediately drawn to Kiyana. "You look beautiful," he said softly, his voice filled with a strange mix of admiration and regret.

But Kiyana's expression was far from beautiful. Her eyes were red and puffy from crying, her face twisted in anguish. "Riyan, let's play truth or dare," she said, her voice trembling.

Riyan's smile faltered for a moment, but he quickly recovered. "Okay, what's the dare?" he asked, his voice laced with amusement.

Kiyana's eyes locked onto his, her gaze piercing. "I dare you to tell me the truth that's held in your eyes, the truth behind all your decent lies."

Riyan's mask began to slip, his eyes darting nervously around the room. But Kiyana's gaze held him captive, forcing him to confront the truth.

"You planned it all, didn't you?" Kiyana's voice was laced with accusation. "You played it well, Riyan. You planned the accident, you messed with my parents' minds, with my medicines... and I always thought you saved me. You were my best friend, Riyan. Why did you do this to me? Why?" she sobbed.

Riyan's eyes welled up with tears, a sight Kiyana had never seen before. "I hated Aarav," he said, his voice cracking. "He was my rival, and I planned the accident for him. But unfortunately, you came and the car hit you... that guilt consumed me, and all I wanted was to see you happy and alive and healthy. But I fell in love with you, Ki. I love you more than words can express."

Kiyana's face twisted in disgust. "You're wrong, Riyan. You don't love me. You love the guilt that's been eating away at you. You love the control you've had over me all these years."

Riyan's face crumpled, his tears falling freely now. But Kiyana's heart remained unmoved, her anger and hurt boiling over.

Kiyana's voice was laced with conviction. "You're wrong, Riyan. When we love someone, we don't chase. Real love doesn't chase; it never does.Love doesn't mean owning that person; true love is letting go. True love is waiting for that person, which is what Aarav did. He waited for five years for me."

Kiyana: "You tried to erase my identity, Riyan. Did you ever consider the life I'd built, the memories that made me who I am?"

Riyan: "I thought I was giving you a second chance, a life untainted by the past. But I was blinded by my own fears. I was wrong, Ki. So terribly wrong."

Kiyana: "A second chance built on deception? That's not love, Riyan. That's manipulation. You controlled my memories, my emotions, my life."

Riyan: "I see that now. I was so consumed by the fear of losing you that I lost myself. And in the end, I lost you anyway."

Kiyana: "You never truly had me, Riyan. Not the real me. You had a version of me that you created, a version that suited your needs."

Riyan: "All I wanted was to see you happy, Ki. Even if it meant sacrificing my own happiness."

Kiyana: "Happiness isn't something you can steal or fabricate, Riyan. It's something that's shared, something that's genuine. You can't manufacture happiness by controlling someone's life."

Riyan's face contorted, his devilish side slowly unraveling. He saw his faults, and Kiyana's tears pierced his soul. He begged, his voice cracking. "Please, Ki, I'm sorry. Don't hate me for all this. Please... I know loving you consumed my inner self. It ruined my ability to see good, and obsession took over. I'm really sorry, Ki". Riyan's eyes pleaded for forgiveness.

"My love for you was a disease, Ki. It infected me, consumed me, and destroyed me. But it also made me human. I never wanted to hurt you. For that, I kept one secret, and for keeping that one secret, I crafted another hundred. It was all my fault."

Riyan's eyes pleaded for forgiveness. "My wish is to see you happy, with me or without me. When you think of me, please don't remember the devil in me. Instead, cherish the friend who loved you,no matter how flawed that love was. But it had nothing to do with you, Ki. I never had the intention of hurting you or doing something against your will, and I never will ". Riyan's face crumpled, his tears falling freely now.

Kiyana's expression softened, her eyes searching for the friend she once knew. She saw the sincerity in Riyan's eyes, and her heart ached.

Riyan's eyes, once clouded by deceit, now shone with genuine remorse. "Let me make things right, Ki. Aarav is waiting for you. I'll take you to him."

That very moment he recalled Aria's words:*we often value something or someone more after it's gone because the pain of loss and nostalgia outweigh the pleasure of having it. At that very moment he realised what he had lost.*

As Kiyana's hands fit into Riyan's, he felt the weight of his regret like a tidal wave crashing down on him. His eyes welled up with tears, and his voice cracked with emotion. *"I'm losing you all over again," he whispered, "but this time, it's not to my darkness, but to your freedom."*

With a gentle smile, he led her towards Aarav, towards forgiveness, and towards healing. As they walked, Riyan's heart bled with a mix of sorrow and relief, knowing that he was finally setting Kiyana free.

....

With a gentle touch, Riyan's fingers intertwined with Kiyana's, his hands holding hers softly as they walked towards

Aarav. The irony wasn't lost on him - he was proceeding to his own emotional undoing, walking in the shoes of a man who was willingly letting go of the one he loved. The bride he had once hoped to claim as his own was now slipping through his fingers, leaving him with a heart full of regret and a soul that was slowly finding redemption.

As she turned to leave, her hand was still clasped in Riyan's. His eyes, once bright with a villainous spark, now shone with a deep sadness. He knew he had to let her go, but it was like tearing his own heart out.

"Kiyana," he whispered, his voice barely audible. His fingers tightened around hers, as if trying to hold on to the moment.

Kiyana turned to him, her eyes filled with a mix of gratitude and apology. "Riyan," she said softly.

With a gentle smile, Riyan lifted her hand to his lips and pressed a soft kiss on her fingers. "You deserve to be happy," he whispered, his eyes welling up with tears. *The power of our emotions is a force so profound it shatters some souls while for others it is where healing is found..*

As he spoke, his fingers slowly relaxed, and Kiyana's hand slipped free. It was like a leaf fluttering away on a breeze, leaving Riyan's hand empty and aching.

The moment seemed to stretch out forever. Kiyana's fingers slid across Riyan's palm, a gentle caress that sent shivers down his spine. His eyes never left hers, drinking in the sight of her, memorizing every detail.

As her fingers reached the edge of his hand, they hesitated, as if reluctant to let go. Riyan's heart skipped a beat. But then, with a soft whisper of skin against skin, her fingers slipped free. Riyan's hand closed into a fist, as if trying to hold on to the memory of her touch.

Riyan thought to himself:

Love leaves fragments, not scars and our story became legend even in its fragments. Love can be a beautiful tragedy but ours was a masterpiece

Kiyana's eyes never left Riyan's face as she took a step back, and then another, until she was standing beside Aarav. Riyan's gaze followed her, his eyes drinking in the sight of her with Aarav.

As Kiyana turned to Aarav, Riyan's eyes dropped to the ground, and he took a deep breath. He felt a pang in his chest, but it was no longer a burning desire to possess Kiyana. It was something more, something deeper.

It was the ache of letting go.

"Letting go hurts, but it's the cost of setting someone free."

"I love you," Riyan whispered, the words barely audible.

But Kiyana heard them. She turned back to him, her eyes shining with tears.

"In the silence of his departure, I acknowledged the cruelest truth: I had given him a glimpse of forever without even intending to stay. And yet, as I watched him walk away, I forgive him... for every hurt, every lie, every shattered promise.

For in his eyes, I saw regret, a deep and abiding sorrow that told me he had finally learned his lesson."

As Kiyana turned back to Aarav, Riyan's eyes followed her, his heart heavy with the knowledge that he had to let her go. But in that moment, he knew that he had found something far more valuable than possession.

He had found the courage to love her selflessly.

As Riyan walked away, he whispered to himself, *"The silence was a mirror, reflecting the damage she had done. Her inability to return my love wasn't a tragedy. The real tragedy was her unintentional act of stealing my trust in it, leaving me to wander a world where love felt like a forgotten language."*

Under starry skies: Forever entwined…

The night sky was a vast, dark canvas, scattered with a million tiny stars, each one a silent witness to their reunion. For five long years, Aarav had carried a hope, a flickering flame that refused to die. He'd waited, never daring to let another heart in, convinced that his "only love " was out there somewhere. And now, here she was, Kiyana, her memories returned, her smile brighter than any star. They sat close, the cool night air a gentle caress.

"Kiya," he whispered, the name, a soft prayer on his lips. "I can't believe it's really you."

Kiyana's eyes, filled with a depth of emotion, met him. "It's me, Aarav,"

A comfortable silence fell between them, filled with unspoken words and shared history. Then, Kiyana reached out, her fingers tracing the line of his jaw. "You waited," she said, her voice barely a whisper.

"Always," Aarav replied, his gaze fixed on hers. "Even when I thought I'd lost you, I knew, deep down, we'd find our way back."

Aarav found himself looking at her, really looking. Not just at her face, but into her. And that's when it hit him. It wasn't just her pretty eyes or her smile. It was the way his own smile reflected back at him from hers, the way her gaze dropped for a second, a little shy, when she realized he was watching. It was like seeing a secret, a beautiful secret just for him.

"What are you looking at?" she asked, her voice soft and a little curious.

Aarav just smiled. "Nothing," he said.

But "nothing" meant everything. *It meant, "I'm looking at you, and you're amazing." It meant, "I'm seeing myself in your eyes, and it's the most wonderful thing I've ever seen."*

A gentle breeze rustled her hair, and a few strands fell across her face. Without thinking, Aarav reached out and tucked them behind her ear. Her cheeks flushed a pretty pink, and she looked down, a small smile playing on her lips.

At that moment, Aarav knew. He knew what people meant when they talked about love. It wasn't some big, dramatic thing. It was this: a quiet night, a soft smile, and the feeling that he could see forever in someone's eyes. It was the warmth spreading through his chest, making him feel like he could conquer anything. It was the simple, perfect feeling of being seen and understood.

The air crackled with unspoken emotions. They leaned in, a silent understanding passing between them. Their lips met in a tender kiss, a soft, gentle promise after years of waiting. It was a kiss that spoke of lost time, of unwavering hope, and of a love that had weathered every storm.

They pulled back slightly, their foreheads touching. Aarav gently tucked a stray strand of hair behind Kiyana's ear, his touch sending shivers down her spine.

"I looked for you," Kiyana said, her voice filled with a quiet strength. "Through every memory, every dream. I knew I wouldn't be complete until I found you."

Aarav pulled her closer, wrapping his arms around her. "You're my universe, Kiya ," he whispered, his voice thick with emotion. "You're everything."

"And now, here we are. Your hand in mine, the cool night air brushing against our skin. I can smell the familiar scent of your hair, a scent I'd carry with me like a secret. Your eyes, they're shining, filled with a warmth that makes my chest ache. Not a bad ache, but the kind that comes from knowing you're finally where you belong.

We've been through storms, you and I. We've faced the kind of darkness that makes you wonder if the sun will ever rise again. But we did it. We found our way back to each other. And in this moment, under this vast, endless sky, I know that everything we've been through, every tear, every moment of doubt, it was all worth it.

Because true love, it's not about fairy tales or perfect endings. It's about fighting for what you believe in. It's about holding onto hope, even when it feels like the world is falling apart. It's about finding your way back to the person who makes you feel like you're finally home.

And you, Kiyana, you're my home. You're my everything. And tonight, under these stars, I know that we'll be okay. We'll be more than okay. We'll be us. Always."

"Love showed me that even in the darkest moments, there's always a glimmer of hope. And that with courage, vulnerability, and an open heart, we can transform our deepest wounds into our greatest strengths."Kiyana said

Kiya leaned into Aarav's arms, her ear pressed against his chest. "Endlessly yours," she whispered.

Aarav's arms tightened around her, holding her close to his heart. "Forever entwined," he breathed, his voice a gentle whisper.

As they stood there, wrapped in each other's arms, the moonlight and starlight above shone brighter, as if witnessing the union of two souls meant to be. lost in the depths of each other's eyes. The world around them melted away, leaving only the gentle rustle of leaves and the soft beat of their entwined hearts. In that magical moment, time stood still, and all that existed was the love they shared. And so, under the celestial canvas of the night sky, they sealed their fate. The pages of Aarav's journal, once filled with longing letters to Starlight, and Kiya's heartfelt whispers to Moonlight, had finally found their happily ever after, a love story etched in the celestial map of their hearts. Their love shines brighter than any star, guiding them into a happily ever after.

True love, like a star in the darkest night, always finds its way. It endures through storms, survives the longest nights, and shines brighter with every challenge it overcomes. Never give up on hope, for the heart that truly loves will always find its way home.

~ *The end*

Beyond the final chapter...

Riyan's eyes wandered, lost in the shadows of his past. Aarav and Kiyana's departure had left a void, but it was Aria's words that echoed within him. She had seen beyond the mask, beyond the devil he had become.

Aria had fearlessly walked into the darkness, her determination illuminating the path. She had seen the real Riyan, the one he had long forgotten. With unwavering conviction, she had pulled him out of the depths, reminding him of the man he once was.

As Riyan reflected on his journey, he realized that Aria had given him a rare gift – a second chance. He had been broken, shattered by the weight of his own demons. But Aria's unwavering faith had helped him mend, and had helped him find his way back.

With a newfound sense of purpose, Riyan stood up, his eyes locked on the horizon. The universe, it seemed, had plans for him after all. Plans that whispered of redemption, of love, and of a future yet unknown.

And as he walked towards the dawn, the shadows of his past slowly fading away, Riyan smiled, his heart beating with a sense of hope. *For in the end, it was not the darkness that defined him, but the light that had brought him back to life.*

When the heart has lost its faith, and love's flame has flickered out. The universe whispers a secret: 'Love arrives when we need it most, in the darkest moments of our soul.

When we can no longer suffer the pain of love, unseen forces conspire to bring us full circle...Back to the beauty of love, but this time, in its divine timing..No regrets, no suffering, just the gentle unfolding of a love that's meant to be.

The universe has a way of weaving its magic, replacing what's lost with something new, yet familiar. Trust that every departure marks a new arrival, and every ending births a new beginning. The universe doesn't take away; it transforms. What seems like an ending is merely a transition to a new chapter. Trust that every goodbye is followed by a hello.

In sixteen moments our paths collided
Nine memories later our bond remains strong
You ignited the spark that fuels my soul deeply always

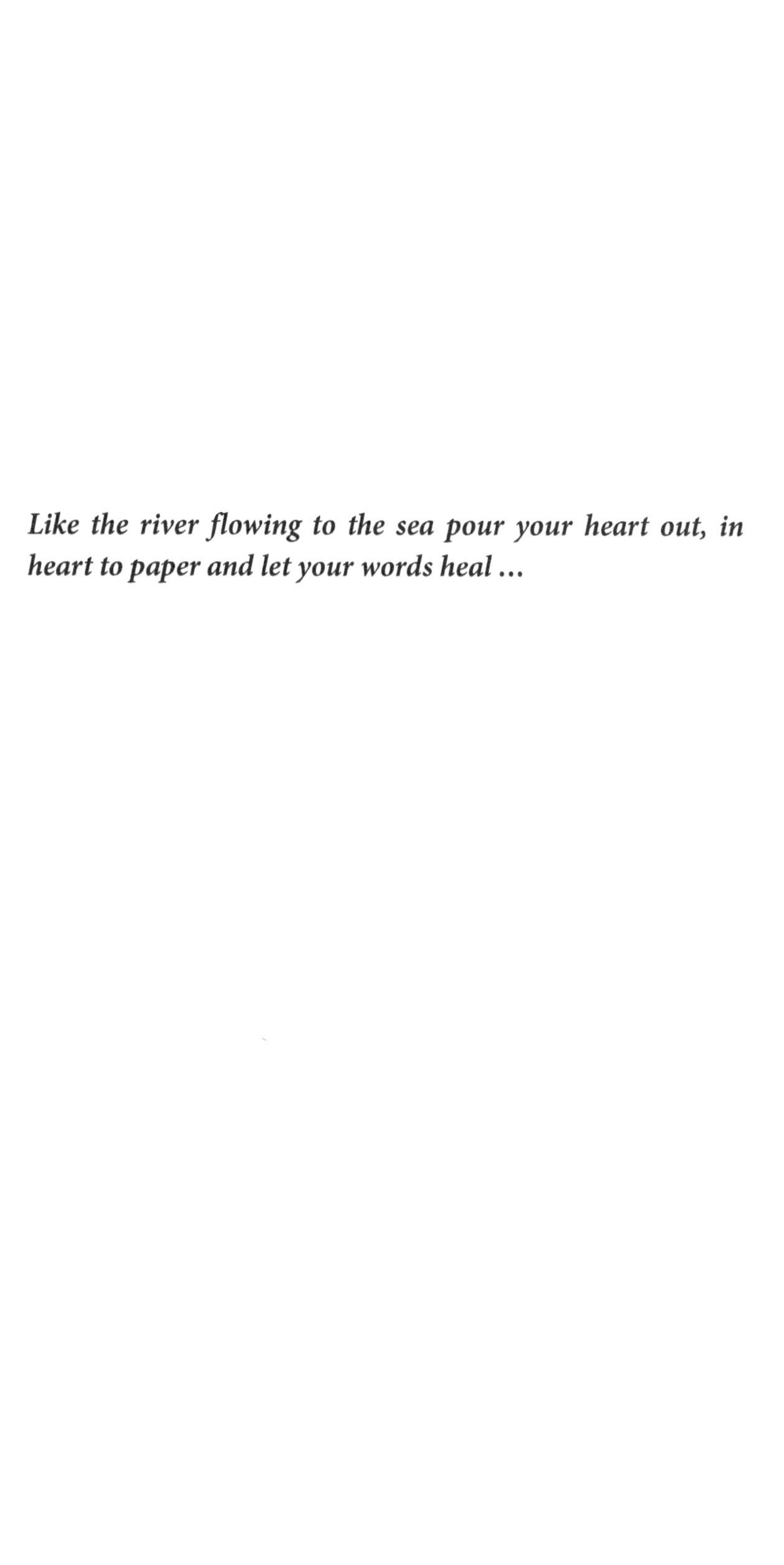

Like the river flowing to the sea pour your heart out, in heart to paper and let your words heal …

Dear Heart,

We're delighted to share our personally curated playlist with you!

These timeless Bollywood classics have been the soundtrack to our love story, and we can't wait for you to experience them!

Grab a cup of chai, get cozy, and scan the QR code below to enter our world of love and melodies!

Happy listening, and thank you for being a part of our journey!

With love,
Aarav & Kiyana

Acknowledgments

As I pen these words of gratitude, my heart overflows with love and appreciation.

To my inner critic, who fueled my pursuit of perfection - thank you for pushing me to soar higher.

To my parents, and my family who nurtured my dreams and encouraged me to chase them - your unwavering support means the world to me.

To my amazing friends, who listened to me go on (and on, and on) about this book, offered words of encouragement, and reminded me that I'm not totally crazy for pursuing this dream - you guys rock!

And to the Divine, who gifted me with the eyes to see the world through the prism of love - thank you for this precious gift. May this book be a reflection of that love, and may it touch hearts and souls in ways that bring joy, comfort, and inspiration.

And a very special thanks to you, dear reader, who's taken a chance on this book and invited its words into your life - thank you for embracing my story. May it resonate with you, inspire you, and remind you of the transformative power of love.

Thank you, thank you, thank you - to each and every one of you who's walked this journey with me.

With love and gratitude,
Kavya